THE PRINCE'S BOY

At the Jerusalem

Trespasses

A Distant Likeness

Peter Smart's Confessions

Old Soldiers

An English Madam: The Life and Work of Cynthia Payne

Gabriel's Lament

An Immaculate Mistake: Scenes from Childhood and Beyond

Sugar Cane

Kitty and Virgil

Three Queer Lives: An Alternative Biography
of Naomi Jacob, Fred Barnes and Arthur Marshall

Uncle Rudolf

A Dog's Life

Chapman's Odyssey

THE PRINCE'S BOY

PAUL BAILEY

B L O O M S B U R Y

NEW YORK • LONDON • NEW DELHI • SYDNEY

Published by Bloomsbury USA, New York
Bloomsbury is a trademark of Bloomsbury Publishing Plc

All papers used by Bloomsbury USA are natural, recyclable products made from wood grown in well-managed forests. The manufacturing processes conform to the environmental regulations of the country of origin.

LIBRARY OF CONGRESS CATALOGING-IN-PUBLICATION DATA
HAS BEEN APPLIED FOR.

ISBN: 978-1-62040-719-6

First U.S. Edition 2014

1 3 5 7 9 10 8 6 4 2

Typeset by Hewer Text UK Ltd, Edinburgh
Printed and bound in the U.S.A. by Thomson-Shore Inc., Dexter, Michigan

Bloomsbury books may be purchased for business or promotional use. For information on bulk purchases please contact Macmillan Corporate and Premium Sales Department at specialmarkets@macmillan.com.

For Marius Chivu

A *heart*: origin of every torment.
E. M. Cioran

And love is love in beggars and in kings.
Anon

One

I ARRIVED IN Paris on Thursday the fifth of May
1927. My father had said goodbye to me two days earlier
at the Gara de Nord in Bucharest. On that memorable
afternoon, I was welcomed to France by my distant cousin
Eduard, whom I had last seen when I was a timid and secretive eleven-year-old. He greeted me in Romanian, embraced
me, and remarked on the grandeur of the Parisian Gare du
Nord where we presently stood.

'Are you hungry, Dinu?'

I answered that I thought I was.

'There's a pleasant brasserie a short walk from here. I had
forgotten how skinny you are. Let me treat you to a substantial meal before I take you to your apartment.'

I thanked him for his generosity.

'You need to stay out in the sun, Dinu. You are far, far
too pale.'

I did not say to Eduard that he might have been echoing my
father, who frequently commented on my unhealthy appearance.
'I shall try to enjoy the summer weather,' I observed instead.

'I shall make it my cousinly duty to see that you do.'

*

We were seated in the crowded restaurant by now.

'Remind me of your age, Dinu.'

'I am nineteen. Just nineteen.'

'Then you will drink some wine with me?'

'Yes. I should like to.'

He ordered a bottle of claret. It would help bring some colour to my ghostly cheeks.

I smiled at this conceit. It had never occurred to me that I looked 'ghostly'. He returned my smile and then we both laughed. 'Welcome to *la vie de Bohème*,' he said when our laughter ceased. 'And please address me as Eduard. Stop respecting me as an elder. Let us be friends.'

'Yes. Yes.'

We shook hands across the table.

Eduard chose the dishes. I ate snails for the first and last time because their rubberiness irritated what I considered to be my discerning palate. I was happier by far with the cassoulet that followed and the *tarte Normande* with which our meal ended. At Eduard's insistence, I had a glass of cognac with my coffee.

'Can you talk yet about your mother, the lovely Elena? You must miss her, Dinu.'

Could I talk about her? What was there to say? She was dead, suddenly and inexplicably dead, and I was having to survive without her warmth and affection.

'Yes, I miss her' was all I felt inclined to reveal. Giddy with drink though I was, and tired after the long journey, my tongue would not be loosened. I had got into the habit of hugging my grief to me as something preciously mine. 'I miss her, Eduard,' I said again, in the hope that he would question me no further.

He didn't. Perhaps he had understood why I was being

laconic, or perhaps he thought I was exhibiting stoicism. That second 'perhaps' would not have been appropriate, since I was anything but stoical. She had died in September 1920 – on the fifteenth of that hated month, to be exact – and I had wept for her in the privacy of my bedroom almost every night since then. I knew, from my cursory reading of Seneca, that stoics are not given to weeping.

'Are you prepared for your bohemian adventure?' Eduard asked as he settled the bill.

'I think I want to write a book. It's my father's idea that I should live the life of an artist in Paris, not mine. He persuaded me to come here.'

'Did you need much persuasion?'

'No, Eduard. Of course I didn't.'

'Cezar is a generous man, but I have never regarded him as especially artistic.'

'He isn't.'

'Which fact makes it more surprising that he should encourage you to stay in Paris, in Montmartre of all places.'

Another cognac was set before me.

'I am drunk, Cousin Eduard.'

'You will sleep the better tonight.'

We took a cab to rue des Trois-Frères, which would be my address until September. I registered the passing scene with eyes clouded by alcohol and drowsiness. Everything was swaying – the buildings, the trees, the trams and buses, the men and women on the boulevards, the late afternoon sun. Nothing in my young world was stable any more.

My generous, inartistic father had secured me a garret, nothing less. Eduard and I carried my two suitcases to the very, very top of the house. This was to be my ivory tower, the ideal setting for a new existence as a poor, striving poet

3

or novelist – I had yet to decide which I would be – whose genius was fated to be unrecognized. No, I was a poet, novelist, genius who could afford to be neglected until posterity claimed me as one of its chosen elite. My paternal benefactor, Cezar, was rich: he had opened a bank account for me; he had paid my rent for the entire holiday; he had made certain that I wouldn't starve. I was going to be an unlikely bohemian, thanks to him.

A plump, middle-aged woman named Simone had led the way up the hundreds (it seemed like hundreds) of stairs. She was the owner's daughter, whom he had entrusted to take care of the property. She would change my bed linen and perform any household duties, such as scrubbing and dusting and laundering, that I required. She hoped that I found the room to my satisfaction.

'Yes, thank you, Madame.'

'I am Mademoiselle.'

She laughed when I apologized for my unintended rudeness, observing that I was the very soul of courtesy.

'My cousin Dinu has perfect manners.'

'It's been a long time since I had a true gentleman lodging here.'

'Did you hear that, Dinu? You must behave impeccably while you are under Mademoiselle Simone's roof.'

'I shall,' I vowed.

I was desperate to sleep. I was trying with difficulty to stifle yawns.

Eduard bade me a fond *au revoir* and the buxom Simone wished me the sweetest of sweet dreams and when they left I cast my clothes aside and fell into the bed she had prepared for me with its starched sheets that smelled of lavender and slept as I hadn't slept since my beloved mother's death.

When I awoke in the late morning of the sixth of May, I felt guilty about her sudden absence from my dreams. I had slept contentedly, and I was remorseful for having done so. I begged her forgiveness and prayed, as I would go on praying, for her immortal soul – for its lasting peace, its rest.

The story I have to tell now is the strangest of my life. I am not even sure that I will be able to account for it. The events I am going to relive and relate took place forty years ago when I was green in the ways of the flesh and the complexities of human intercourse. Let me say, simply, that the writer-to-be Dinu Grigorescu was innocent about the random nature of everyday living. He was happy in his attic or garret, looking down on the bustling city and thinking only of putting words, immortal words, on paper. The people below were as nothing to the youthful genius. He was in possession of the tidiest of ivory towers and it was from that well-scrubbed hideaway that he would send out his messages, in verse or prose, to an appreciative or incurious public. He anticipated both praise and scorn, for he knew already that artists of his calibre were born to be recognized by the discerning few and rejected by the legion of philistines whose facile judgments always held sway. That much he understood. That was, almost, the extent of Dinu Grigorescu's knowledge.

I spoke French with increasing confidence as the first weeks went by. Eduard's business had taken him to London so there was no one with whom I could converse in my native tongue. I was content with this. I felt like a true Parisian whenever I passed for one in lively exchanges with street vendors, waiters, bar keepers, cab drivers, tram conductors and shop assistants. To complete the disguise, I bought a beret and wore it at an angle that might be described as jaunty.

The blank sheet of paper in the attic stayed blank. I had words in my head and there they remained. I was waiting, I suppose, for inspiration. I hoped it would come to me in a sudden rush, as it had come to Rimbaud and Eminescu, my Romanian god, and Mozart, and all the geniuses I emulated. I had to be patient, I told myself as I drew my father's money out of the bank. I had to – what was the phrase that was in the air? – 'sit pretty'. Yes, I was 'sitting pretty', and I could do so with a certain confidence because I was still a teenager. I had June, July and August ahead of me. It seemed like all the time in the world.

It was on the afternoon of Thursday the twenty-sixth of May that I met the man I would know for ever as the prince's boy. He was not a boy any longer, since he was already approaching middle age. I can now relate, without embarrassment, the peculiar circumstances in which I encountered him. I had eaten lightly and drunk somewhat heavily that lunchtime and had left the restaurant in a state of sexual excitement. The human fruit I was desperate to devour was of a much forbidden kind – nothing less than a crime against nature and a cardinal sin in the eyes of my Orthodox faith. The claret boiling in my veins was leading me towards the ideal object of my desire, first sighted in the form of a railway porter when I was twelve years old. The unknown workman, who had winked at the blushing boy whose bags he was carrying, was strong and hairy and free – I supposed – of any melancholic feelings. I paid him the pitifully few *lei* it was the custom to give public servants and was desolate when he shook my hand and turned his back on me and went off in search of another customer. I watched his retreating figure until my parents accused me of ignoring them. I collapsed into my mother's embrace and wondered as I did so if I could ever tell her of the strange and terrifying emotion that was still possessing me.

(Of course I couldn't. I had worshipped the porter for at most five minutes in July 1920 and on the fifteenth of September she was suddenly, inexplicably dead.)

The porter, or someone very like him, perhaps stronger and hairier, was in my thoughts as I walked – not too unsteadily, I hoped – towards the Bains du Ballon d'Alsace. I had heard tell of the notorious place from a drunken policeman in a bar near rue des Trois-Frères who had said, in the loudest of whispers to one of the waiters, that Monsieur Albert's establishment was providing all the men in Paris, married or otherwise, who enjoyed something different – he emphasized the word – everything they craved for a hundred francs. If Albert charged the clients a hundred francs, what was he paying the queer young men who satisfied the lepers and degenerates who were in need of their disgusting services?

This leper, this degenerate, listened and took note of the address the gendarme was now broadcasting to the entire room. Dinu Grigorescu could just about afford a hundred francs for an experience that might lead him to write like Maupassant or Baudelaire or his adored lunatic Rimbaud. He would send a letter to his father with the news that he was spending Cezar's money wisely. Such was the leper's lustful reasoning as he strolled along rue Saint-Lazare on that sunny afternoon.

I entered the paved courtyard, decorated with bay trees and privets in large terracotta pots, and hesitated. What on God's earth was I doing? I could easily turn round and walk away. I was on the point of doing so when the glass-paned front door with the word BAINS emblazoned on it opened and a smiling man emerged.

'Are you one of M. Albert's new recruits?'

I replied that I did not understand his question.

'You innocent little rogue,' he said. 'You pretty minx. What is your name?'

'Jean-Pierre,' I answered. 'Jean-Pierre,' I repeated, as if to convince myself of my chosen identity. 'I am Jean-Pierre, Monsieur.'

'I shall ask for you next time. I shall put in an order for you, Jean-Pierre.'

I thanked him. What else could I do, or say? I ascended the four steps leading to M. Albert's establishment and found myself looking into the cold blue eyes of its owner. He was seated behind a heavy cash box. Have I written 'seated'? I should more accurately write 'enthroned'.

'Are you seeking employment?'

'No.'

'How old are you?'

'Twenty-one,' I lied.

'Do you propose to be my youngest-ever client?'

'I assume so.'

'What do you call yourself?'

'Jean-Pierre.'

'Preposterous. Your French is good enough but it is not natural French. You hail from somewhere else in Europe. Permit me to make a guess. Hungary? Poland? Not, heaven forfend, Romania?'

'Yes.'

'Are you of noble blood, my black-eyed boy?'

'I have never been told so. My father is rich, however. He is a successful, a highly successful, lawyer. He has been employed by our king and queen.'

'Why have you come here? What are you doing here?'

I was silent. I could not give expression to my inexpressible desire.

'My expertise in all matters carnal informs me that a sensitive creature is invariably attracted to a brute. I have a brute on the premises, as it happens, and he is not engaged with a gentleman at this moment.' He stared at me. 'Is it a beast you require?'

I stared back. 'Yes,' I finally managed to reply. 'Yes, it is.'

'That will be a hundred francs, Monsieur. Your real name, if you care to disclose it, will be safe with me.'

Safe? 'I am Silviu Golescu,' I told him.

'You will be enjoying the services of Honoré. He is a beast beyond compare. Allow me to lead you to him.'

I followed M. Albert up a flight of stairs. There was a corridor with three cubicles – nothing grander – on either side. In the second on the left sat Honoré, waiting for work. He was smoking a Turkish cigarette.

'Honoré, my dear,' said Albert. 'This is Jean-Pierre. Treat him gently or brutally, according to his wishes. I entrust the rich young gentleman to you.'

Honoré grunted thanks to his employer and commanded me to sit beside him on the bed. Albert closed the door discreetly.

'You are young,' Honoré remarked. 'Are you a virgin, Jean-Pierre?'

I said nothing.

'That means yes.'

'Yes.'

He took my hand and stroked it. I froze in terror.

'You are very nervous, Jean-Pierre. You are very, very nervous.'

The more he spoke to his terrified customer, the more I became convinced that he wasn't French.

'Yes, Honoré. You must forgive me but I *am* frightened.'

'There is no reason to be. Your eyes are as dark as mine.'

'Are they?'

'Yes. I will show you my body. I will remove my clothes for my frightened Jean-Pierre.'

Within seconds, he was naked. I marvelled at his hairy beauty. I gasped and gawped and was transfixed.

'Now show me yours.'

'I am too skinny, Honoré. I am ashamed to show myself.'

'Then let me undress you.'

He did so, gently and swiftly. He held me to him and kissed my forehead. He squeezed me until I was breathless.

'You are a child,' he whispered, releasing me. 'A naughty, naughty child. Does your mother know what you are doing?'

'My mother's dead.'

'Did you love her?'

'Yes, yes. I still love her. I will always worship her.'

'That is good to hear, Jean-Pierre. That is very good to hear.'

I knew now, by listening to him, that he was a pretend Honoré, just as I was a pretend Jean-Pierre. We were impostors.

He embraced me again and ran his fingers along my spine. His hand finally rested where I wanted it to rest.

We kissed for the first of many times that summer. I was startled by what I was doing with such eagerness, such warmth, such abandon. I should have been kissing a girl of my own age, in a drawing-room, perhaps, or by a tennis court, but not in a cubicle in a male brothel under the guise of a bath house. What in God's holy name was happening to me? And why was I allowing it to happen?

'It is nice to have a sweet young man beside me instead of an old lecher.'

'Is it?'

'Yes, yes. Let me explore my pale little peach.'

He explored me. That is all I am compelled to say as I set down my Parisian adventures in the spring of 1967, in the days or weeks or months that are left to me. He explored Jean-Pierre. That is all, and that is everything I care to remember for the present.

Spovedanie – that is the word we Orthodox Romanians use for 'confession'. The morning after my meeting with the 'beast beyond compare', I found a heavily incensed church in a side street near the Bastille where I sought out a priest who would be willing to listen to and, perhaps, comfort me. He was bearded, of course, as all Orthodox priests are, and before he listened to me he remarked on my youth and the impossibility of my having anything serious to confess.

What did I crave his, and the Lord's, forgiveness for? I made no mention of the pretend Honoré and the place where we met. I muttered something about being in the possession of overpowering lust. I was in thrall to it, I told him. I was enslaved to it. I wanted to be released from its tenacious grip.

I recall that he was silent for some minutes after I had finished speaking. His reply, when it came, was measured.

'You are young. The feelings you have described to me are normal, alas, for a man of your age. You must attempt to resist them. Resisting the irresistible will be a great challenge for you. I entreat you to face that challenge.'

I assured him I would. I would suppress the feelings until I met the woman I would marry and love and cherish. Would, would, would – how easily I employed the word; how cavalierly.

I told the truth to my mother that evening before I went to sleep. I told her everything about Jean-Pierre's meeting with Honoré. I told her, in a whisper, how he had explored me and how strangely wonderful that exploration was.

In bed, between the starched and lavender-scented sheets, I began to weep. God, in His infinite wisdom, knows why I did, for I had no knowledge myself. I surrendered to the insistent tears. I gave in to a grief it was impossible to comprehend.

I was awoken by birdsong at dawn. I said my morning prayers and heard myself apologizing to my irreplaceable mother for my brazenness. As I washed and dressed, I vowed that Honoré, whoever he was, was out of my life now. Let him continue his sordid activities without me. Let him be the plaything of rich, elderly lechers. Let him be out of my sight and out of my thoughts. Let him be gone.

I went to my writing table and stared about me, waiting for inspiration, my pen in my eager hand, until Mlle Simone knocked on the door and startled me out of my reverie.

'There is a letter for you, M. Dinu.'

It was from my cousin Eduard. He had booked tickets for *Les Folies Bergères*. The phenomenal Josephine Baker, who was the toast of Paris, was on the bill that very evening. I was to dress smartly and be ready on the dot of eight. He promised to do his cousinly duty and take me to dinner after the show.

The phenomenal Miss Baker was a Negro, as were all the musicians who accompanied her. She was the star in a piece called The Plantation. She and her troupe were all happy slaves, for I have never seen, before or since, so many pure white smiles on any stage. Josephine rolled her eyes, wriggled her bottom and tap-danced whenever the mood suited her. She wore the tiniest of shorts, displaying long and agile legs. I enjoyed the performance, even as I was mystified by it.

'Why is she considered phenomenal?' I asked my cousin when we were seated at a banquette in Café Larivière.

'She is such a free spirit,' he answered. 'She has made her home here because the enlightened Parisians are indifferent to a person's colour. You cannot imagine her singing and dancing in Bucharest, can you?'

No, I couldn't, I replied.

'What has the young genius been writing?'

'Who is that?'

'You, of course. How many pages have you filled?'

'A few. Just a few. Only a few.'

'Cezar is expecting nothing less than a masterpiece, Dinu. You must try not to disappoint him.'

'I shan't,' I said, and added 'I hope.'

'My dear, dear cousin, he is expecting nothing of the kind. He simply wants you to see the world and enjoy life while you can. I recommend the *boeuf bourguignon*.'

Towards the end of the meal – after oysters and champagne, and the beef, and an entrancing blood-orange sorbet – I was tempted to tell Eduard about my encounter with the swarthy Honoré. I knew it would be insane to mention him even, but at that moment there was a madness in me that needed to find expression, in however indirect or opaque a form.

'You are your mother's boy, aren't you, Dinu?'

'I love my father, too,' I assured him, without much conviction.

'There is another mother's boy who is a great writer, I am reliably informed. His name is Marcel Proust.'

'I have been meaning to read him.'

'I think you should. Perhaps it might encourage you to write about Elena. I hear that Proust's mother was sparing with her affection, unlike the woman who stroked and petted and worshipped her one and only Dinu. She is foremost in your thoughts, as we both know, and I don't believe you will be a novelist or poet, or whatever it is you want to be, until you have discovered a way of coping with her loss. That is my considered, cousinly advice.'

This story that is the strangest of my life really began that evening in Café Larivière. My adventure with Honoré was a prelude, an overture, to the drama that would soon take place. I heeded my cousin and went out the following morning and bought the first two volumes of Proust's labyrinthine novel. Reading of the narrator lying alert in his bed, unable to sleep until his mother blessed him with her soothing presence, I accounted myself fortunate in being the son of Elena. Marcel – I assumed it was Marcel – had no such good fortune. He had to wait for his conciliatory goodnight kiss, whereas I received as many kisses as Mamă felt like bestowing upon me, and sometimes there were many. My grief in 1927 was that of a young man who had known maternal love; his unhappiness, I began to understand, was made more poignant because of the terrifying element of doubt. He had wanted her to demonstrate her abiding affection, not to say devotion, for him, but her demonstrations were brief and inadequate. There were guests to entertain downstairs and it was important that she joined them. A single quick kiss, little more than a peck, would have to be sufficient. It was never, ever enough for him. It would constitute a lasting absence in his life.

I purchased three more volumes. I read them in my ivory tower, in cafés, in parks. I had discovered a complicated

– oh, how complicated – soul mate. I wrote to my father that Proust was the writer, above all other writers, I wished to emulate. He replied on a postcard that he hoped I was well and happy and enjoying the unique pleasures of Paris.

There was one unique pleasure I wished to enjoy once more, despite my vow not to see or think of him again. The exploratory talents of the man I knew could not be called Honoré were beckoning me back to the house on rue d'Arcade. On two occasions I walked to the corner of the street and found myself incapable of venturing further. I heard the priest chiding me; I fancied I caught my mother sighing; I listened to what I thought might be my conscience warning me of the dangers ahead. The voices caused me to retreat, to retrace my steps to rue des Trois-Frères and the comfort and privacy of my attic and yet more chapters of Marcel Proust.

'Welcome to my Temple of Immodesty,' said M. Albert. 'I was certain you would make a return visit. I know that Honoré, my irreplaceable Honoré, will be pleased to see you.' He flashed his faded teeth in a smile as he added: 'It is Honoré you want, is it not?'

'It is.'

'I shall wake him presently. If he has a failing, it is that he sometimes indulges in wine and other alcoholic beverages to excess. He arrived for work this morning in a most dishevelled and unhappy state. I was so perturbed by him that I nearly disposed of his services. I was on the point of slamming the door in his face when I instantly thought of you, my dear young rich Romanian, and the disappointment you would feel if he wasn't here on the premises to satisfy your every delightful and wayward desire. Your appearance today is, I declare, something akin to a miracle.'

'How long must I wait?'

'Be patient. Try and cool your ardour. Make yourself comfortable on Mme Proust's chaise longue while I conduct an investigation into Honoré's physical and mental condition. I shall tell him you have arrived and are anxious – I think "anxious" is the right word – to see him.'

He had darted out of sight before I could ask him if the chaise longue on which I was seated had really belonged to a Mme Proust. It was covered in a light green material that had seen better days a forbiddingly long time ago. Was 'Proust' a fairly common name in France, I wondered.

'He is washing and shaving and preparing himself for his sweet Jean-Pierre, alias Silviu Golescu. You are Silviu Golescu, are you not?'

'Of course I am.'

'Of course you are.'

'Who is, or was, Mme Proust, M. Albert?'

'Oh, such innocence. Mme Proust is the mother of the novelist –'

'Marcel?'

'There is no other. Yes, yes. M. Marcel Proust considered it an honour to have gained my friendship. When I opened my first indecent establishment, he presented me with some unwanted items of furniture that had once belonged to his parents – such as the chaise longue on which your cherished bottom is currently resting. It was extraordinarily kind of him. He has been dead five years, but I often imagine that he is here with me, particularly on Wednesday afternoons, when the monstrous Russian Safarov reduces a ludicrously wealthy, and unashamedly common, industrialist to a bleeding, gibbering wreck. Oh, the screams, the excitement. I have dukes, princes, counts among my clients, but it is only that vulgar man and his need for the brutal Safarov who keeps me in business. It pains me that this should be so, M. Golescu, but it is nevertheless the truth. Allow me to show you what I call the Vatican Library.'

The Vatican Library, which was housed in an upstairs room above the reception desk, contained volumes of the *Almanach de Gotha* and *Burke's Peerage* and several books on heraldry, and nothing more.

'The aristocracy is my passion, Silviu Golescu,' he explained. 'And their foibles, their peccadilloes. For me, they are like manna from Heaven. I seek them out and make them my own.'

The doorbell rang. M. Albert advised me to stay where I was, among the crowned and titled heads of Europe.

He reappeared with the news that another, richer, titled gentleman was demanding an hour, at least with – he was embarrassed to inform me – Honoré.

'I shall go then,' I said. 'I cannot compete for his favours.'

'No, no, M. Silviu, I insist on your staying. There is no competition, I do assure you. Nothing so coarse. You are Honoré's preferred one, anyway.'

'Am I?'

'That is what he confided in me. You are favoured.'

I parted with a hundred francs, which M. Albert had the courtesy not to count. He poured me a glass of fine sherry, from the estate – he hastened to inform me – of a Spanish marquis who was a devout connoisseur of the pleasures M. Albert's unholy Temple provided.

I sat in the Vatican Library and listened to its bald and pudgy librarian as he regaled me with stories of his former beauty. 'My hair was golden. Nothing as common as blond. Prince Radziwill was not alone in remarking that I looked like an angel with my flowing locks and azure eyes. Alas, I am a fallen angel now, I fear, for ever excluded from the paradise the young and beautiful inhabit. I function on the periphery of paradise, you might say, where I am able to bring Honoré and Jean-Pierre together in happy union, as I trust I shall be doing within the hour.'

He consulted his pocket watch and clicked his tongue in annoyance.

'Within the hour, yes.'

Another, louder bell sounded from below.

'Ah, the clarion call of duty. That will be him. He is prepared to see you at last.'

He was standing in the doorway of his elected cubicle, smoking a Turkish cigarette as before and smiling on me as I stumbled into his presence.

He greeted me, softly, in Romanian. In an instant, he had ceased to be Honoré. I cast Jean-Pierre aside for ever when I replied to him in the language we shared by birth.

'I have missed you, my pale one.'

'And I you,' I heard myself admitting. 'And I you.'

He pulled me into the tiny room and held me to him, kissing my hair, my ears, my eyes, my nose, my lips in what I understood to be a frenzy of passion.

'My name is Răzvan.'

'I am Dinu.'

'Truly?'

'Truly. And you are truly Răzvan?'

'I am. Believe me.'

I said I believed him. I was glad we were no longer impostors. I was happy beyond all words to be with him again, to be his Dinu. I said all this as his arms encompassed me.

It was an afternoon of mutual, tender exploration. I was a navigator, too, with every spot, every blemish on his body subjected to my determined, microscopic investigation. His pimples and warts and blackheads were mine to worship. They were among my treasured possessions now. I shared a cigarette with him, the first of many shared cigarettes, afterwards. Oh, that word 'afterwards', suggestive as it is of both satisfaction and desolation. 'Afterwards' came to mean something final to me, a last parting of the ways, long before Răzvan and I became estranged. I hated the very idea of 'afterwards', wanting our love-making to happen in a perpetual present.

It is love I am writing about here, in this memoir of a life half-lived. I have mentioned the railway porter and my inexplicable longing for him and his re-emergence as Honoré and then Răzvan. I have documented as a fact that I was drawn in my youth to men who were hairy and muscular, who represented a manliness denied me by nature. That fact, which alarmed and mystified me in the summer of 1927, causes me wry amusement now, for the brute I met in squalid circumstances on May 26 of that fateful year was none other than a prince's boy, the adopted child of a man of exquisite refinement, who had shaken the limp hand of Marcel Proust and mingled with artists I could only dream of meeting. Răzvan, at the age of thirty-eight, had entrancing stories to tell the pale beauty whose heart he was happy to possess. My explorer became my teacher in those habits and ways of the world I was unable to imagine or conjure up at the writing table in my pristine attic.

'I have much to share with you, my sweet,' he said softly. 'This will be the last time we meet in M. Albert's house of sin. From tomorrow, you will be my guest at the apartment the prince purchased for me.'

'Prince? What prince?'

'You will discover who he was soon enough.'

'Why can't you tell me now?'

'Not now. Not here. It is a long story and I need to stay calm to make sense of it. If I ever can, Dinu. If I ever can.'

I yielded to him again, at his encouraging insistence, and was soon in the timeless space that only lovers inhabit. And then, satisfied, we slept in each other's arms until M. Albert woke us with the message that someone very distinguished was requiring Honoré's services.

'I have finished work for today. I am going home. Inform the gentleman that Honoré is tired and unable to cope with his demands, whatever they may be.'

'You are breaking my rules. You are not showing me the respect you should.'

'I shall be leaving with Jean-Pierre as soon as we have washed ourselves.'

'You are acting irresponsibly.'

'I am not a machine, M. Le Cuziat. May I remind you that I am not a machine? Even you cannot make me do what you want me to do by order.'

The speechless M. Albert glared at the naked Răzvan, who kissed me and said:

'You may not believe it, you snobbish pimp, but I have fallen in love.'

We stopped at a bar where the waiters knew Răzvan. They greeted M. Popescu as an honoured customer.

'This is Dinu, my new friend from Romania. He has come to Paris to write a book. He is a very romantic young man.'

Răzvan ordered a large bowl of mussels and some bread to soak up the juices.

'And the Sauvignon de Sainte Brie.'

He found subtle ways of touching me across the table, convincing the other drinkers and diners that he was like a father to me, if not my father himself. I revelled in the deception. I was even tempted to call him Tată, whenever his fingers stroked my arm or ruffled my hair.

'What I said to Satan is nothing but truth, Dinicu. I am in love with you. Hopelessly, I think.'

Dinicu – that old diminutive from a bygone age was the name my mother gave me. I last heard it on her lips as she lay dying on the fifteenth of September 1920.

('Oh, my dearest Dinicu. I have to go away from you, my son. You must trust in the Lord. We shall be together again one day.')

'I seem to have upset you with Dinicu. Will you be my Dinuleţ instead?'

'That is so childish, Răzvănel.'

'This is baby talk, Dinuleţ.'

'But aren't I your baby, as the Americans say, Răzvănel?'

'You are Dinuleţ, you are.'

Răzvan walked me home to the house on rue des Trois-Frères which boasted my ivory tower. It was a balmy evening, I remember. Mlle Simone, wine glass in hand, was in the street, talking and laughing with another concierge. She saw her lodger and his companion approaching and ran towards us.

'My dear M. Dinu, you must introduce me to the very handsome friend you have been hiding from us.'

'I haven't been hiding him. I did not even know he was

in Paris until I met him by accident a few days ago. We lived close to each other in Bucharest,' I lied convincingly.

'Let us celebrate your reunion then.'

And that is what we did, in a nearby bistro, with Simone and Françoise, for another hour or so. Răzvan, drinking more wine than all of us, suddenly became incapable of coherent speech, in either French or Romanian. He muttered that I was his sweetest Dinicu, which I hoped and prayed they didn't understand.

'Where does he live?' Mlle Simone asked me.

'On the other side of Paris,' I answered. 'Would it be possible–?' I began the question but was too embarrassed and shy to continue.

'Go on.'

'Would it be possible for him to pass the night in my room?'

There was a silence, during which I think I froze with the terror of immediate castigation and rejection.

'Of course it is possible. You will be uncomfortable, I predict, but it is certainly possible. Oh, just look at him – he's already asleep.'

Mlle Simone held his left arm, I his right, as we laboured to guide him up the Everest of stairs that led to my attic. I loved her in those precious, awkward moments as surely as I had ever loved my mother.

'I shall leave you to undress him, my dear. I shall bring you coffee – a great deal of coffee for him – and croissants in the morning.'

I managed to undress him, though he tried to fight me off, thinking perhaps that I was someone else, and hauled him into my bed, and nestled in the arms I dexterously contrived to wrap around me, for the entire blissful night. I couldn't sleep as I lay beside my snoring and farting and occasionally garrulous Răzvan, out of sheer wondrous happiness. I kissed all the blemishes that now belonged to me, every blessed one of them.

'What's that smell, Dinicu?'
    'It's lavender.'
    'Where am I?'
    'In my room, Răzvan. In my bed, to be precise.'
    'How did I get here?'
    'Heaven knows.'
    'That's no answer.'
    'You were very drunk and very tired. You walked with me to Montmartre from M. Albert's Temple of Immodesty. We stopped for moules marinières on the way. You told me many times that you love me. You met Mlle Simone and Mlle Françoise and drank glass after glass after glass of your favourite claret. Mlle Simone and your beloved – I hope, I hope – Dinicu or Dinuleţ dragged you upstairs. And here you are, beside me. Is that a satisfactory answer?'
    'It will do.'
    'It's the gospel truth, Răzvan.'
    'I need to piss, sweet one. I have a tremendous need to piss.'
    I showed him where the nearest tiny room was, on the landing one floor down from my ivory tower.
    He returned to my arms. We savoured each other's garlicky breath. There were parts of our bodies we hadn't previously explored, but we did so now. We were quiet in our endeavours, out of respect for Simone, who was waiting below with coffee and croissants, we hoped.

*

We talked about our mothers to begin with. His was called Angela, as befitted her angelic nature. Răzvan was the youngest of her four children, born a month and a day after his father's death.

'My brothers and sister were old enough to work on the estate. That is how our family survived.'

'Which estate? Where?'

'You are very curious. You want to know everything, don't you?'

'Everything, yes. And more.'

'It's in a place you will not have heard of. It's in a remote part of our great country.'

From the age of six, or was it seven, he too was toiling in the fields, digging up potatoes and turnips and picking apples and plums off the trees. He went to school twice a week, learning his alphabet and his numbers, and listened to the stories about fairies and goblins and evil spirits his mother, Bogdan, Mircea and Irina recounted to him. Angela was the best of all storytellers, frightening him in the sweetest and gentlest ways by reminding him that everything she said was make-believe as she tucked him into his bunk with a goodnight kiss. She always made the sign of the cross, to ensure that the Holy Ghost would take care of the Răzvan who was not to know a father's love.

'I want to hear about Elena.'

To my astonishment, I was tongue-tied. I might have been with my cousin Eduard, not the man with whom I was infatuated. I struggled to find the words that would convey the depth of my feeling for her. All I could say, at the start, was:

'She was beautiful.'

'Oh, Dinu, all mothers are beautiful, even when they

have the faces of cows or pigs. You are a clever boy, my dear one, who reads Marcel Proust. If I tell you that Angela has lost every tooth in her head but is still glowingly beautiful in my eyes, you will have a picture of her. Describe Elena to me, you wretchedly inadequate writer.'

I had revealed to him that I was waiting for inspiration. The moth or butterfly had yet to break free from the caterpillar and spread his wings wheresoever he wanted.

'Now tell me, dearest caterpillar, what kind of woman Elena was.'

'Is. She is still in my thoughts.'

'I should hope so. I am anxious to learn more.'

'She lived,' I said, to my surprise, 'in the shadow of my father. He is a forceful, clever, opinionated man. His name is Cezar and he could easily have been a Roman emperor. My mother never contradicted him, never doubted his word. Once, when he wasn't there with us, she begged me to try to forgive him.'

'Forgive him, Dinuleţ? For what?'

'I did not understand then and I am not entirely certain that I understand today. I assured her that I would forgive Tată because he was my Tată.'

'Was he cruel to her?'

'He wasn't warm or loving to her, as you are to me.'

'Has he been cruel to you?'

'No, no. I am here in Paris, thanks to him. It's due to his generosity that I have met you. The two hundred francs I paid M. Albert were his. I think I can say that Cezar Grigorescu has been excessively kind to his one and only son.'

Răzvan's apartment on rue de Dunkerque, in which he had lived for thirteen years, was sparsely furnished. There were framed photographs on the tables on either side of his bed and icons of St Nicholas and the Virgin on the walls. These added colour and mystery to the otherwise drab room we transformed, from June until September, into our universe.

'Who is that man with the moustache?'

'He is no ordinary man. He is my prince. He's handsome, wouldn't you say?'

I think I shrugged.

'Is my Dinuleţ jealous?'

'Why should I be?'

'Because you love your Răzvănel passionately, blindly, and blind and passionate lovers are invariably jealous.'

'He doesn't look happy to me.'

'Happy? My prince? He had little cause to be happy. It's true he was rich and had privileges and was free to travel anywhere in the world he wished, but his smiles were so rare they surprised you.'

'Did you love him?'

'I honoured him, Dinu. I shall always honour him. If you are asking me if we slept together the way I sleep with you, the answer is no. I was a simple boy when he adopted me and a clever boy when he died. I owe my cleverness to him.'

'What kind of cleverness?'

'My elegant French. My knowledge of church architecture. My appreciation of beauty in the form of Domnule Dinu Grigorescu – these are the hallmarks of the cleverest of men.'

'You sound convincing.'

'We are no longer in business, you and I, as it happens.'

'What do you mean?'

'You do not have to pay me – and by "me" I am referring to Albert Le Cuziat – for my services. They are services no longer. My love for you cannot, and should not, be bought and sold.'

'I am flattered,' I said. I wanted to say more – I wanted to say much, much more – but found it impossible to speak.

'I am looking at you and reading you like the book you haven't written yet and perhaps will never write. You are wondering why a cultivated man has been working in a professional capacity for the devilish M. Albert, yes?'

'I could be.'

'I know you are, and I adore you for being curious. I have some questions for you, too. Between now and September, we shall enjoy many illuminating conversations. At this very moment, I am feeling lonely and abandoned lying here. Please join me.'

I joined him.

One morning, days later, I woke up in my lavender-scented bower and knew despair of the blankest, bleakest kind. I write 'knew' because I seemed to be beyond feeling. I was in possession of a knowledge I could not begin to fathom. It was there, inhabiting my body. It was telling me that I would never weep again, however much I felt the desire to. I had entered, overnight, an unfeeling universe.

I had been taught that Hell was a place for the restless, that their dissatisfactions would continue into eternity. I wasn't restless now; I was numb. I was no one. I had a name, Dinu Grigorescu, but it was without meaning or significance. I could as well have been called a stone or a cabbage.

I could as well have been dead.

'Cezar instructed me to thank you for your letters,' Eduard said the next time we met. 'He is a very busy man, Dinu.

He is dealing with a case that occupies every one of his working hours and some of those when he should be sleeping. He was on the telephone for five minutes at most. I told him you are in good health and content with your bohemian life. I was right to do so, wasn't I?'

'Absolutely right.'

I said nothing of Răzvan, of the pleasure he afforded me, for I was Dinu Grigorescu again, the prince's prince's boy, and no longer a stone or cabbage. I had passed the night in my beloved's bed, from which I had risen reluctantly as the bells of a nearby church struck noon.

'Have you made any friends, Dinu? Or acquaintances?'

This was the occasion to be inventive. I could see that he was genuinely curious and was suddenly desirous to satisfy his curiosity.

'Many, Cousin Eduard. Many friends and acquaintances.'

'Tell me about them.'

'We could be here a long time if I described each and every one. This *poulet à l'estragon* is delicious.'

'So it should be, at the price they are demanding. I am listening, Dinu.'

He listened, seemingly enthralled, as I ran through the names of totally imagined bohemian friends. They were aspiring painters, musicians and poets, but there were others who had no artistic ambitions at all. I spoke of Michel and Yves and Celeste, of Raymond and Jacques, and – this was daring of me, for it tested my cousin's knowledge of Proust's novel – a certain M. Vinteuil, a composer of densely subtle chamber works, to whom I had been introduced by a man from Brittany, who knew everyone in Paris it was worth knowing.

I paused for breath, amazed at my daring. Vinteuil? Albert? I waited to be exposed as the charlatan I was.

'For such a shy and reticent young man, you seem to have developed a remarkable capacity for friendship. You have truly blossomed in Paris, Dinu. I congratulate you.'

The fraudster in me refused to be contained.

'I have met someone who once shook hands with Marcel Proust,' I said, stating a truth at last. 'He tells me Proust's handshake was very limp.'

'Who is this privileged person?'

Why, it was Răzvan, my solicitous cousin Eduard, I did not say. It was Răzvan, whose spell I am under, whose arms I have deserted to be with you.

'A man I met at the Opéra, at a performance of *La sonnambula*. It was one of those chance encounters.'

'Ah, yes. What would our lives be without them? Did this gentleman give you his card? Will you be seeing him again?'

'I doubt it.'

'That is a pity. I should have enjoyed meeting him.'

'Perhaps our paths will cross one day. Paris isn't so very large a city.'

'You have more colour in your cheeks, Dinu. You no longer resemble a ghost. Your healthy complexion must be due to the food and wine you eat and drink with such evident relish.'

'It's possible,' I said. 'I have a strong appetite for the finer things in life these days.'

The finest of them being Răzvan, whose name I wanted to pronounce in the unmistakeable voice of love. My appetite for Răzvan is the strongest of my appetites, I acknowledged in silence.

'Cognac, I think.'

If there is a single phrase guaranteed to bring my once

dear, justifiably dead cousin Eduard back before me it is 'Cognac, I think.'

Beneath the icons of St Nicholas and the Virgin Mary, my true, and lasting, education began.

'You must promise not to interrupt me.'

'I promise.'

'You will be the first and last person to hear my story as I wish to tell it.'

I nodded, for fear already of interrupting him.

'Which means, my dear one, that you will have to be patient with me.'

He was staring at the carpet, I remember now, with his head in his hands, waiting – I supposed – for something akin to inspiration to strike him. I waited, too, with the patience he demanded of his worshipper.

'It seems so long ago. I was eleven, Dinu, when the prince first noticed me. It was a summer's day, as it is now, and I was weeping, to my shame, because my mother had slapped me for disobeying her. The prince saw me and stepped down from his landau. He asked me, in his refined Romanian, why I was unhappy. I had no words for him. How could a peasant, a serf, have words fit for a prince? I know I wiped my tears away, but I remember little else except for my embarrassment.'

He smiled at me and fell silent. His recording angel, for such I already considered myself, waited for him to continue.

'The prince advised me to be cheerful and said that he desired to know my name. I answered that I was Răzvan Popescu, the son of Angela and Ilie Popescu, and brother of Bogdan, Mircea and Irina. They were alive, and my mother was also, but my father was dead. I had never seen him, because he had died before I was born.'

It was towards the end of the summer, at harvest time, that the prince appeared in the doorway of the modest shack the Popescus called home. Răzvan's mother curtseyed on seeing him, but he told her such a courtesy was misplaced as he pressed her hand in his. He wished to speak to her in private in his house on the estate. He had an urgent matter to discuss with her before returning to Paris in September.

What could this 'urgent matter' be? It was very mysterious, a man of his noble birth wishing to meet with one of his peasants in the privacy of his grand mansion.

'The prince's valet served my mother tea, much to her mortification. The mystery began to be solved when the prince observed that her youngest child, the boy who had entered the world without a father, had impressed him with his polite and gentle way of speaking.'

He paused, catching – again I supposed – my disbelieving look.

'Yes, Dinicu, the words are mine and far beyond the limited extent of my mother's vocabulary. The sophisticated Răzvan is trying his best to convey her confused feelings as the prince made his unexpected proposal to her in August 1901. His proposal was as simple as it was preposterous. He wished to adopt me, to educate me, to transform the boy Răzvan Popescu into a man of substance.'

What happened next, he said, would be revealed later. It was time to make love, and then it would be time to eat and drink.

Perhaps this is the book I could not write in Paris in 1927 or in Bucharest in the 1930s, or in the lonely decades that followed. I was inspired – ah, that word 'inspired' – by a dream in which the railway porter of July 1920 carried my bag out of the station and joined my parents and me in the family car. Cezar and Elena smiled on the youth as he held their son in his plebeian embrace – a demonstration of genuine affection from one who might be described as the 'salt of the earth' – and dared to kiss him. They were entranced, or seemed to be, by the youth's boldness. It was then, as the lips of Dinu Grigorescu brushed against those of the for ever unnamed porter, that Elena said, 'I shall die happy now, Dinu. I shall die very happy two months from now.'

If my mother did indeed die happy, it was not in the knowledge that her only child had found a replacement for her affections in the love of a hirsute railway porter with neither money nor prospects. This much her grieving Dinicu understood within minutes of awakening from the worst of all bad dreams.

'You must trust in the Lord, my darling Dinicu.'

'I will, Mamă.'

'For the rest of your days.'

'Yes, Mamă, I promise.'

It is a promise I have attempted to honour for her sake, though often with difficulty, for forty-seven years. I am putting my limited trust in Him now, I think, as I continue writing about those I loved and tried to love in two European cities that once resembled each other.

Răzvan would stay in Corcova for another year after his bewildered mother at last accepted the prince's strange proposal. A tutor was found to refine his Romanian and teach him French. The lessons with Alin Dănescu, a prematurely silver-haired graduate from the University of Timişoara, took place in the library of Prince E's grand house.

Doctor Dănescu was a rigorous teacher, unsparing with his sarcasm when the student inevitably made mistakes.

'Oh, stop insulting me with your foolishness, young Popescu. It is tiring for me to even attempt to teach someone who knows so much more than I do. Let us reverse roles. Educate me, if you please, *mon maître*, in the eternal art of idiocy.'

Răzvan scowled. Răzvan glared at his teacher. Răzvan did not respond or reply to Alin Dănescu's taunts, for he realized – this simple peasant boy, who had yet to sit, enraptured, in a theatre – that the man with the slightly twisted mouth filled with insults was an *actor*, a pretend-person. He was like one of those men who impersonated angels or demons on feast days. He was putting on a show.

They read the stories and memoirs of Ion Creangă together and the poems of Mihail Eminescu in those early lessons. Under Alin Dănescu's tutelage, Răzvan Popescu blossomed into literacy. Within six or seven months, the prince's boy, as he was known now to peasants and servants alike at Corcova, had progressed to the *Fables* of La Fontaine. There came a day, an important one for the attentive student, when Răzvan asked the momentarily startled Alin Dănescu if he had instructed him sufficiently in the 'eternal art of idiocy'. Răzvan had phrased the question in his new-found French, to his own delight and his tutor's surprise.

'You rascal. You rogue. You devil.'

They became friends at last, and would remain so for years.

'Do you still see him?'

'Only in my mind's eye. He's dead. My mind's eye, when not clouded by drink, is constantly occupied. It sees into hundreds of dark places, my dearest.'

I lay beside Răzvan, beneath the icons, listening as he described his unusual schooling, of a kind the railway porter was denied, and marvelling, as I'd continue to marvel, at my absurd good fortune.

'I am a leisurely storyteller, wouldn't you say, Dinicu?'

'You are.'

'I enjoy keeping you in suspense.'

'You appear to.'

'But not for much longer. All will be revealed by the time you return to our homeland. How far into the future is that? Eight weeks? Seven?'

'Eight, I hope. Eight, I sincerely hope, Răzvănel.'

I bought the remaining volumes of Proust's novel, a book so complex and subtle that it dulled all my silly inspirational aspirations. I knew nothing, then, or very little, of life beyond the confines of Dinu Grigorescu, and yet Proust appeared to be aware of everything diversely and peculiarly human. My admiration for Marcel Proust coincided with my love for Răzvan Popescu, the prince's boy who had shaken the master's limp hand. I encountered them both in the final days of May 1927, when I was eager and ready to be beguiled. I suppose I have lived in that state of beguilement ever since.

'I have cast a spell on you,' he said one morning, when I was too besotted to contradict him. 'I have entrapped you with my magic powers.'

'Yes, you have.'

'You are silly if you believe that.'

'Then I am silliness personified.'

The days till September were running away from us. There was no time left for arguments, even pretend ones of the kind he was proposing. I made it clear to him with my body that I was in need of love.

'You are a greedy young man, Dinicu.'

'I can't deny it.'

Our mutual hunger once assuaged, I lay in his arms and begged him to go on with his story.

'Where was I with it?'

'You are still in Corcova, with your tutor, speaking French.'

'Ah, yes. But not for long. That autumn I was removed – I think that is the appropriate word – to Paris. Alin accompanied me to this address.'

He paused. He sighed.

'And then Alin returned to Timişoara and I was honoured with a smart new tutor – an assistant professor at the Sorbonne. And the prince sent me to a tailor who specialized in English – or should I say Scottish? – tweeds. Within a matter of weeks, my dearest Dinicu, I was a young man about town. I was dapper from head to toe. I would dine with the prince in the back rooms of discreet expensive restaurants and sometimes, but not often, in his apartment in the family's grand house in Île de la Cité.'

I held my breath before I asked if I could be sure that the prince and he had not made love.

'I have been anticipating a repetition of that question for days. You must understand, my insanely jealous sweet one, that the prince loved me. He loved most of all the *idea* of a peasant boy who could speak perfect French and move and act with grace. I was, I suppose, his creation. We never explored one another, Dinu Grigorescu, if that is what you wish to hear.'

I lacked the courage to say it was. My silence caused him to smile.

'I have made my happy one happier, I can tell. And yes, I was in awe of my prince for taking me away from the fields of Corcova and allowing me to live a charmed and civilized life. Yes, yes, yes. Yes, and again yes. That is enough of my revelations for today.'

It was on the third Saturday in August that I next met up with my cousin Eduard. He was even more welcoming than usual, embracing me fulsomely when I arrived at the table in Café Larivière. He ordered vintage champagne – 'Cezar is paying for everything today' – and announced that there would be greater treats in store for me.

'Why?'

'No questions, if you please. Let this be an afternoon of pleasant surprises.'

'But why?'

'Let us just say that your generous Tată is exceeding himself in generosity.'

I wanted to ask why a third time because I was mystified by my cousin's decidedly theatrical behaviour. He seemed almost too happy in, and with, the role he was playing.

'We are booked in at four o'clock.'

'Booked in? Where? At a theatre?'

'A theatre of sorts.'

'The circus?'

'Not exactly.'

'The opera? The ballet?'

'Oh, Dinu, this entertainment is superior to all of those.

I insist you believe me. Have faith in your Cousin Eduard.'

The champagne disposed of, we took our first sips of a glorious Château Palmer. Oysters were followed by brill, the brill by grouse – 'The first of the season' – and the grouse by a selection of black, blue and red autumnal fruits.

'That was truly a feast, Eduard.'

'As it should be, on such an important day. Cognac, I think. We shall have one each and nothing more. We have to perform as best we can, and drink may diminish the quality of our performances.' He winked at me. 'There must be no diminution this afternoon.'

'Eduard, you are drunk.'

'Am I?'

'Yes, you are. You drank most of the champagne and almost all of the claret and I suspect you weren't sober at the start of the meal.'

'Coffee will solve the problem. The *temporary* problem.'

'I shall go back to my attic and try to work. I have to return to Bucharest with a few written pages, at least.'

'No, no, Dinu. The pages are of no consequence. What matters to Cezar is that you accept his gift, his precious gift, this very afternoon. We must honour our engagement in twenty minutes.'

'Must we?'

He consumed more coffee, paid the exorbitant bill, and asked the head waiter to hail a cab for us. He named an address off the Bois de Boulogne.

'They know me as M. Gérard, so please do not look surprised,' he said when we arrived at our destination.

The driver, to whom my tipsy cousin gave a lavish tip, told us we were lucky devils. He wished he was a man of leisure with money to burn.

'What did he mean, Eduard?'

'You will soon be enlightened.'

The door was opened by a maidservant, who curtseyed as we entered.

'Madame Laurette is expecting you, M. Gérard.'

We followed her into a salon. My eyes took in a heavily bolstered sofa, covered in plum-coloured velvet, a large gilt-framed mirror and a potted palm.

'Ah, my dear M. Gérard, it has been too, too long since you last honoured us with your presence.'

A tiny woman, with dyed orange hair, appeared from behind a silk screen.

'Yes, Mme Laurette, it has been far, far too long. I am a very busy man. My business leaves me little time for the unique pleasures you offer.'

'That is sad to hear. You will allow Denise to offer you her special brand of consolation?'

'Never doubt it, my dear Madame.'

'This pretty youth is the cousin you spoke of?'

'He is, indeed. Permit me to introduce you to Alexandru.'

'Good afternoon, Alexandru. You have the name of a warrior.' Her laugh was surprisingly deep for such a frail, even skeletal, woman. 'Perhaps you are a warrior, too.'

'Perhaps,' I responded, thinking suddenly of Răzvan, my own Alexander or Xerxes. 'Perhaps.'

'You are a fortunate young man, Alexandru. The utterly exquisite Sonia is all prepared for you.'

Sonia? All prepared for me?

'I shall take you to her, Alexandru. My dear Gérard, you do not need me to remind you where to find Denise. Come with me, you handsome beast.'

38

Why did I go with her? Why didn't I apologize to Mme Laurette and to my cousin and leave the scented house immediately? The 'utterly exquisite Sonia' was for other men, not Dinu Grigorescu.

Mme Laurette mistook my embarrassment for nervousness. She patted my hand and told me to summon up my courage. It was natural that I should be agitated. Sonia would soothe and charm the anxious warrior.

'Sonia?'

'Yes, Madame?'

'The Romanian gentleman is with me. He has the looks of Rudolph Valentino.'

'Bring him in this minute.'

Sonia was wearing a pearl-coloured dress that stopped above her knees. I saw her clothes before I registered her elfin beauty.

'I will leave you to your loving ways,' said Mme Laurette. 'Be brave, Alexandru.'

Sonia wondered if I cared for a cigarette. I replied that I didn't.

She sat on the bed and invited me to join her. I answered that I was happy enough standing where I was.

'Were you in Paris when Mr Charles Lindbergh landed his aeroplane in January? What a remarkable achievement, don't you think, to fly all alone across the Atlantic?'

'Very remarkable, to be sure.'

'I am yours, Alexandru, if you want me.'

'I don't want you, Sonia. I can't want you.'

'You are not the first shy boy to say that. Would you like to see my breasts?'

'No, I would not.'

She rose from the bed and moved towards me.

'Is there another shy boy in there?' she asked as she attempted to undo my trouser buttons.

It was then, to her astonishment and mine, that I began to weep. I had glimpsed, if only for a second, the eyes of Elena Grigorescu in Sonia's face – those eyes that had always looked on me benignly were a trapped animal's now, signalling terror.

'There's nothing to be afraid of.'

'Yes, there is. Yes, there is,' I all but screamed. 'I have to leave this place. I have to go.'

'You are booked for an hour,' she stated, matter-of-factly. 'That was the arrangement.'

'My father's arrangement, not mine. Cezar Grigorescu will pay your bill, if he hasn't done so already.'

'I hate to see you upset,' she whispered. 'You poor soul.'

'Yes, that is exactly what I am. Let me kiss your hand at least.'

'Please do.'

'I shall leave you quietly.'

'You are still crying.'

'I know I am. I shall stop soon. I can't bear to stay here a moment longer. I feel imprisoned.'

'Goodbye.'

'God bless you,' I said and closed the door behind me. I ran down the stairs, out of the house and along the busy Bois de Boulogne, playing a carefree game in which I managed to flit past the late afternoon shoppers without touching or bumping into them. My well of tears had dried up. I was rushing towards Răzvan, the first deep love of my life.

'You are sweating, Dinuleţ, and you are out of breath and you look as if you have seen a colony of ghosts. What is the matter with you?'

'Shall I tell you? Everything?'

'Not in gasps, my sweet. Calm yourself. I can already guess what you will say to me will be amusing.'

'My cousin took me to a brothel near the Bois de Boulogne.'

'Ah, yes. It's world-famous, Dinu. That old crone Laurette caters for ambassadors and visiting royalty as well as politicians and businessmen. How much did you pay her?'

'You tease me. I paid her nothing. My father settled the bill. It was his gift to me.'

'What a kind man he is.'

'Do you know Mme Laurette?'

'She is a fixture of Paris. She isn't such a snob as our friend M. Albert because money is more important to her than rank. She is not a personal acquaintance, Dinu.'

'She looks like a witch.'

'Did she frighten you?'

'Yes.'

I accounted for the eternity I spent with Sonia. I described her dress, her jewellery, her hair and the bangs on either side of her head. I recalled that she had mentioned Charles Lindbergh and that she had tried, and failed, to unbutton my trousers.

'It's amusing, as I predicted.'

'I broke down, Răzvan,' I protested. 'I wept. I screamed at her.'

'I hope you apologized for your childish behaviour.'

'Have you no sympathy for me?'

'Did you apologize to her?'

'I kissed her hand.'

'Then I have sympathy for you, my dearest. I sympathize with you completely. Let us pray that your father, the beneficent Cezar, will be as sympathetic as I am.'

'I have wasted his money.'

'He may be angry with you for doing that.'

'He will be,' I predicted, accurately.

He reminded me, then, that he had something to offer me that it wasn't in Sonia's power to give. I was to come to him and accept it, this very minute.

I was happy, as ever, to do as I was bidden.

I heard nothing from my cousin for almost two weeks and there were no messages or postcards from my father. Răzvan guessed rightly when he observed that my failure with Sonia was indicative of a greater failure. I had disgraced, or dishonoured, the manhood of the Grigorescus. I had shamed the family with my perverse behaviour.

I finished reading Proust and then I started reading him again. The accusatory blank sheet of paper on the writing table had lost its power to accuse me of idleness or lack of discipline. I had discovered my literary hero and I intended to devote my contemplative life to him and whoever I might find to be his fellow spirit if not equal. That was my ambition now.

'Do you remember the fallen angel?' Albert Le Cuziat asked me as I stepped out of the bank one morning.

'Of course I do,' I answered. 'Monsieur Jupien.'

'You recognized me in Marcel's portrayal?'

'I did, indeed. To the life.'

'That is not a particularly flattering thing to say, my dear Domnule Silviu. But it is fame of a kind, I suppose, to be immortalized under another name. Have you withdrawn enough money to invite me for coffee at the Ritz?'

'I think I have. Shall we get there by cab?'

'You are a beauteous, courteous, handsome Romanian.'

I was enjoying this chance encounter so far, even though I was vaguely aware that Albert had some cunning scheme in mind. There was a game about to be played and I was anticipating it with a relish that both startled and exhilarated me. There was entertainment of a curious kind ahead, I suspected.

All was decorous to begin with, as befitted our opulent surroundings. The waiters brought us Italian coffee and dainty glasses of iced water and a selection of exquisite little savouries and pastries.

'I do so appreciate gracious living, Silviu.'

'It is my pleasure to provide it.'

I waited for my guest to mention Răzvan. He had said nothing about him as yet.

'When do you return to Bucharest?'

'All too soon, I fear. At the end of September.'

'Are you feeling homesick?'

'No, not in the least. I think I have come to regard Paris as my spiritual home.'

'Only spiritual?'

'Shall we say *partly* spiritual?'

'My first inamorato was a priest. He was a Breton, like me. He understood all too well the battle that rages between the flesh and the spirit. My golden loveliness, if I may indulge myself in a moment's immodesty, captivated and tortured him. I put the poor prelate on the rack, I must confess to you.'

'Tell me more.'

'Only at your insistence.'

'I insist.'

'He had a past, my father confessor. Do you understand

what I mean by a past? You are, perhaps, too young to have had one.'

'I hope I am wise for my years, M. Albert. I believe you are referring to matters of a physical, as distinct from a spiritual, kind.'

'You are a clever, peach-bottomed boy. Oh, by the bye, one of my regular gentlemen is completely smitten with Jean-Pierre, the *nom de guerre* you assumed on the day you plucked up all your reserves of slightly inebriated courage to set foot in my Temple of Iniquity. He saw you hesitating outside and was totally enchanted by your black eyes and pale complexion. The sentiment is his; the description is mine. He has a title and is richer than most of the European aristocrats whose tarnished lives are my speciality. He would delight in crossing your palm with as many pieces of silver as you desire.'

'I am flattered.'

'He is obsessed with his Jean-Pierre. I have scoured Paris for pretty minxes to satisfy him, but none of them has afforded him the delicious pleasure he hopes and prays you will give him.'

'Are you soliciting on his behalf, M. Albert? I cannot believe you are. My heart, as you must surely know, belongs to another. Isn't that the appropriate, romantic cliché?'

'I am sorely afraid it is. Love is such a hindrance to business. Lust and obsessiveness are infinitely more conducive to financial stability. I have ceased being a practising Catholic, Alexandru – oh, wicked me, did I really say Alexandru? – but I find myself making the sign of the cross on Wednesday afternoons as soon as Safarov arrives to satisfy the over-eager tycoon. Safarov is my devilish saviour. His brutishness enables me to keep the police at bay and my bank manager contented. I thank God there is no danger of his falling in love.'

'You called me Alexandru.'

'Did I? Yes, yes, I did. My partner in sexual crime, Mme Laurette, informed me that a certain Romanian gentleman matching your description visited her renowned premises in the company of an older man. She said you gave your name as Alexandru, Silviu.'

'Yes, I did.'

'You were, perhaps, in a conquering mood?'

'I wasn't, Albert. I was terrified. The episode convinced me, though I did not need convincing, that I belong to Răzvan, or Honoré, as he was when I first caught sight of him. We are lovers. We adore one another.'

'So I feared. Love is such a time-wasting condition, Silviu. I bade it adieu as soon as my hair fell out. It exhausts your talents. I am talking, I trust you appreciate, about romantic infatuation, the malignant disease that blights the lives of the perpetually young. You will recover from your enchanted episode with Honoré – oh, do forgive me, Răzvan – when you are safely back in Romania. These are my wise words for you. Heed them, pretty one. I should be pleased to accept your invitation to luncheon, if such a kind thought has occurred to you.'

'Would you care to join me for luncheon, M. Albert?'

'What a delightful surprise. I should be honoured. In case you had not noticed, today is Wednesday. The dreaded Safarov is not expected until five o'clock. Shall we eat and drink at a leisurely pace?'

'That is an admirable suggestion.'

My guest was known, in some cases well-known, to the waiters in the restaurant at the Ritz. They greeted him

45

effusively and welcomed me, too, with quite unusual friendliness.

'They are assuming, my dear Domnule Silviu, that you are of noble birth. I only dine here with dukes, counts, princes and their like. I would never be seen here, dead or alive, with the wealthy industrialist. My reputation as a man of taste and discernment would be in tatters otherwise. He dresses well enough, at all-too-obvious expense, but his essential vulgarity cannot be concealed by silk and cashmere. Let us toast him, never-theless, Silviu.'

'Must I?'

'Oh, yes. It is thanks to him that you were able to enter my Bains d'Alsace and meet your beloved. I am dependent, I regret to admit, on his largesse.'

'How can I raise my glass to a man with no name? Am I toasting a phantom?'

'No, no. He is real. He is composed of flesh and blood. Let us call him, for convenience, Nemo.'

'To M. Nemo,' I said.

'Amen.'

'Is it your belief,' I inquired of my limitlessly snobbish acquaintance, 'that I shall remain perpetually – I think you chose the word "perpetually" – young?'

'Unless you come to your senses, that is indeed my belief. Enjoy to the full the sorrows of young Werther before you attain the age of thirty and then cast them aside for ever and a day. Do that and give yourself the opportunity of living a reasonably contented life thereafter.'

'You sound very serious and more than a little pompous. Do you regard Albert Le Cuziat as a contented soul?'

'No, no, not at all. I wish to God I were,' he said, making

the sign of the cross again. 'But I do hope you will achieve happiness.'

'So do I.'

'I wish, Silviu, I wish most earnestly, that I had refrained from introducing you to Răzvan. He is a tortured creature.'

'Tortured?'

'Indubitably. He will transport you to hell with him under the name of love.'

Albert Le Cuziat conveyed these bad tidings with a smile I would describe as pitying. His alert eyes and nicotine-stained teeth were united in conveying the message that my adoration of the prince's boy was the merest folly.

'I have no evidence of his being, as you say, tortured.'

'That is because you are besotted. You are seeing what you want to see and nothing more.'

The renowned, or notorious, M. Albert and his distinguished, if not entirely aristocratic, host were then presented with the finest dishes the Ritz's chef could offer: a sublime lobster bisque; lamb with an apricot stuffing; a ripe Camembert and raspberry, strawberry and lemon sorbets. M. Albert chose the wines, which were – predictably – expensive.

'This is a rare indulgence for me, Silviu. It is a pity Răzvan is not here with us.'

'Is it such a pity? I sense you are being ironic or sarcastic or ambivalent.'

'You listen well.'

'I look at faces, too. When the words coming from your mouth do not match the expression in your eyes – your twinkling eyes, M. Albert – I become aware of a certain insincerity.'

I wanted to know more about the prince's character, beyond the fact that he had shown inordinate kindness to my lover. Răzvan had told me little of any consequence concerning him, I lied.

I waited a long time for an answer.

'I am not lost for words, I do assure you. I am weighing them, placing them in the correct order. You speak of the prince's kindness. It is not a characteristic of the man I knew. He was far from kind to his friends and relatives when he killed himself in a cheap hotel in a drab suburban town in England ten years ago. I have retained enough of my Catholic faith to assert that I consider suicide a sin – a sin composed of vanity and cowardice, to put it precisely. His death reduced the dry-eyed Marcel Proust to tears; it left his doting, admiring brother bewildered and heartbroken, and his cousin horrified at his cruelty.'

'And Răzvan?'

'He felt abandoned, naturally. He had lost a civilized companion and a brilliant teacher. He was stranded, Silviu. He moped. He began to drink. It was impossible for him to return to Corcova. The prince and his money had refined the peasant boy out of recognition. Try to imagine him toiling in the fields.'

'I can. I can easily picture him at harvest time.'

'You have smelt his cologne?'

'I have.'

'You have appreciated his impeccable French?'

'His impeccable Romanian, too.'

'You are absurdly starry-eyed. So Răzvan is your noble savage, is he? He is such an inappropriate choice.'

I seem to recall that we finished the meal in silence. Then he anticipated the question I was too frightened, or too jealous, or too despairing to ask.

'He has been in my employment for seven years.'

'Has he?'

'Yes, Silviu.'

'You must be pleased with his work.'

'I was pleased with him when he was capable of performing his duties. He would often disappear for weeks or even months, depending on his mood.'

'Did he enjoy working when he was, as you say, capable?'

'Enjoy? Dear God, no. He hated – oh, why am I speaking in the past tense? – all his customers. Some of them were excited by his rage and happily returned to be insulted, but others were appalled by his insensitive behaviour. Răzvan's is a sophisticated cruelty, thanks to the prince's tutelage. Tell me, Domnule Silviu, has he been cruel to you?'

'He has no cause to be.'

'Allow me to make a confession. I gave Jean-Pierre to Honoré as a gift – to placate him, to soothe his savage breast. He thanked me for my kindness. He thanked me so frequently and so much on the days he was pining for you that I cursed myself for my uncharacteristic generosity. Oh, Silviu, what a fool I was to show him kindness.'

'I am exceedingly grateful that you did.'

'Your feelings are understandable at the moment.'

'May I accuse you of cynicism?'

'You may. It is an accusation I can neither challenge nor refute.'

There was a curious relationship developing between us – a friendship, almost; a marriage of unlike minds. I did not tell him I found his company diverting, since there was no cause to. I had made it apparent with smiles and nods and spontaneous bursts of laughter. I could not picture him as my enemy, despite his regret at having introduced me to Răzvan.

'I am drunk, M. Albert, but you do not seem to be.'

'I have willed myself to remain clear-headed. It is a talent I have mastered in the service of my chosen profession. I cannot afford to be inebriated on a day of gladiatorial sexual combat. I am referring, you will recall, to the imminent liaison of the timid industrialist and the merciless Safarov. Would you care to witness the bloody spectacle? There is a peephole in the wall of the torture chamber. I have only to remove the minute landscape painting that conceals it for you to have an uninterrupted view of the grisly proceedings. I had a similar peephole in my previous establishment for the sole benefit and satisfaction of my dear departed Marcel.'

'I thank you for the generous offer, M. Albert, but I rather think I prefer to be where no blood is shed.'

'As you please.'

'You cannot tempt me into being even more wicked than I am already.'

'So you consider yourself wicked, do you?'

'Yes. And perhaps, no. It was bad of me, seriously bad of me, to visit your sinful establishment. But my love for Răzvan, and his for me, is—' I hesitated before saying the word '—sacred.'

'Ah, my dear, you make such a fine distinction between the disorderly house and its saintly occupant. Such a very, very fine distinction.'

I settled the astronomical bill, the very last astronomical bill of my life, while thanking Cezar Grigorescu for allowing me to be so profligate.

We descended the steps outside the hotel – I shakily; he with enviable assurance – into the street.

'My name is Dinu Grigorescu,' I said to Albert Le Cuziat

as he entered the cab the doorman, whom he tipped ostentatiously, had hailed for him. 'That is who I am.'

'In vino veritas, Dinu Grigorescu. My compliments to the treacherous Răzvan.'

I returned to the prince's boy's apartment and slept the sleep of the satiated beneath the benevolent icons of the Virgin and St Nicholas. I was awoken hours later by Răzvan, who freed himself from the uniform he was now constrained to wear as a barman at *Les Deux Cygnes*.

'What did you do today while your lover was in respectable employment?'

'I met M. Albert. He seemed to be waiting for me outside the bank. He invited himself to luncheon at the Ritz and I decided to accept his invitation.'

'You paid?'

'I paid.'

'You fool.'

'I paid for him out of gratitude, for introducing us to one another. He proved to be an amusing guest.'

'Being an amusing guest is one of his talents. He does not have many, but that is certainly one of them.'

'Come to bed, my love. I am lonely here.'

'Did he mention me?'

'Hold me in your arms and I will tell you.'

I waited until he had done my bidding before I answered.

'Yes, he did mention you. He thinks you have betrayed him. He considers you to be treacherous.'

A long silence followed and then Răzvan was spluttering with laughter.

'Oh, Dinicu, he says I am treacherous. That is wonderfully funny.'

'Is it?'

'Of course it is. The old snake has the effrontery to accuse me of treachery. This man is a cheat and a liar beyond compare.'

'I am sure he is. Let's forget him now.'

It was an impossible request. Entwined together in bed, we banished him from our thoughts, we imagined, as we embarked on another exploration of familiar territory. We made love. We made love in defiance of Albert Le Cuziat, our Pandar, our cold-eyed matchmaker.

'I beg you not to see him again,' Răzvan whispered as we shared a cigarette. 'He is poisonous, my sweet one. His tongue drips poison. Please keep away from him. If you love me, do as I ask.'

'There is no "if",' I assured him. 'There won't ever be an "if", I promise you.'

I was with Răzvan when I saw my cousin Eduard again. We were sitting, hand in under-the-table hand, outside a café near rue des Trois-Frères.

'Good evening, Dinu. Did I hear you speaking Romanian with this gentleman?'

'You did, you certainly did,' I answered, putting my hands on the table. 'Good evening, Cousin Eduard. Allow me to introduce you to a new-found friend of mine – Răzvan Popescu.'

'I am pleased to make your acquaintance, Domnule Popescu.'

'And I yours.'

'May I join you, Dinu? Or are you discussing urgent private matters?'

'Of course you may join us, Cousin. You are most welcome.'

I hoped that my excessive politeness would disguise the embarrassment I was feeling.

'Do you speak French, Domnule Popescu?'

'He speaks perfect French, Eduard. His way with the language is a pleasure to listen to.'

'Dinu is very generous with his praise, Domnule Grigorescu.'

'Vasiliu. My name is Eduard Vasiliu.'

'My apologies.'

'There is no need for them. Your glasses are empty. Do you have a taste for champagne, Domnule Popescu?'

'I do indeed.'

'Then that is what we shall drink.'

Cousin Eduard was clearly intent on impressing Răzvan, for the champagne he ordered was of an expensive vintage.

'Did you meet here in Paris or in Bucharest?'

'In Paris,' we replied, almost in unison.

'Tell me more.'

It was Răzvan who rescued us.

'I met your cousin Dinu on an overcrowded tram. The passengers were pressed together, like sardines or anchovies in a tin. It was unbearably stuffy and people were losing their tempers. Dinu was so exasperated that he cursed very loudly in our language. I echoed his fierce sentiments in a gentler tone of voice and from that moment we were friends.'

Răzvan answered the questions Eduard seemed to hurl at him with a calmness that could only dazzle me. Nothing was said of Corcova and his poor peasant origins. He was a native of Cluj, he declared. His father, now alas dead, had been a schoolteacher, and his mother, a gifted dancer, still taught the rudiments of ballet to a group of impossibly thin little girls who aspired to be Tchaikovsky's cygnets one day.

'Were you eligible for military service in 1914?'

'I assumed I was eligible to fight, but the examining

board, in their ancient wisdom, decided I was not. I have
flat feet, Domnule Vasiliu. It is a sadness to me that I was
considered unfit to be a soldier.'

'Those are noble words.'

'You fought for the Allied cause, I trust?'

'Old as I look now, I was just too young then.'

'That is a pity. I was expecting to hear that you had been
awarded a *croix de guerre* or some Romanian medal, at least.'

'No, no – I am not cast in the heroic mould. I am a busi-
nessman. My sole interest is in amassing money.'

'Which you are spending on your nephew and his friend
with exceptional generosity.'

'It's not exceptional, Răzvan,' I interrupted. 'It is
customary.'

'Is it?'

'Decidedly so. My cousin is like my father in that respect.
It pleases him to be generous when the mood seizes him.'

'Domnule Popescu, are you entirely certain that you
encountered Dinu on a crowded tram?'

'Entirely.'

'And not at the Opera, during a performance of *La
sonnambula*?'

'I tend to fall asleep during *La sonnambula*. I have, I fear,
made a regretful habit of it. The crowded tram represents
the dreary truth, doesn't it, Dinu?'

'It does,' I agreed.

'So be it,' said my disbelieving cousin.

Two

I HAD A photograph of Răzvan with me on my return to Bucharest. I had no need to look at it for the moment because the smell of him was with me, enticingly with me, as the train made its uncaring progress across the dreary Hungarian plains. I kept hearing his voice, insisting that ours was only a temporary parting – once reunited, we would never be separated again. Yes, I answered aloud, to no one and anyone.

I was met at the station, the ersatz Gare du Nord, by Gheorghe, the family chauffeur. He doffed his cap to me and welcomed the young master home. The fatted calf had been killed in my honour and his wife, Denisa, was already in the kitchen preparing it for tonight's feast.

'I hope there will be some of it left over for the servants.'

I promised him that I would eat sparingly, though I could not guarantee that my father's guests would do the same.

We lived in one of the city's smartest streets, near Cişmigiu, overlooking the park of that name. The Grigorescu house was grand enough to be mistaken for an embassy. Cezar Grigorescu was not contented, as his fellow lawyers and distinguished acquaintances were, with an apartment, however large. He demanded a mansion in which to strut

55

and assert his authority. Carmen Sylva 4 was his ideal pala-
tial residence. I entered it now with something akin to
loathing, remembering the attic in which I had pretended
to write and the rooms the prince had rented for my lover.
My lover. I stood in the hallway, picturing him beside me,
the welcome guest of my father and my mother's shade.

'You must be Dinu,' said a voice I did not recognize. I
turned and saw a woman dressed in a similar fashion to the
girl who called herself Sonia to the boy pretending to be
Alexandru. 'I am Elisabeta.'

'Are you?' I answered, stupidly.

'You have not heard of me?'

'Not a word.'

'Nothing at all?'

'Absolutely nothing. Should I have heard of you?'

'Yes.'

'Why is that?'

'Your father has not told you?'

I was beginning to enjoy this game of questions and
counter-questions.

'No, Elisabeta, my father has not told me whatever it is
he should have. He has kept me in ignorance on the subject.'

'I am very surprised.'

'Are you? Why?'

'Because his failure to tell you something so important
makes no sense to me.'

'He must have a reason for keeping his son in the dark.
The word "failure" is not in Cezar Grigorescu's lexicon. He
is a man accustomed to making decisions.'

'Of course he is.'

I ended our mysterious conversation by stating the truth.
I was tired to exhaustion after a long train journey on which

I had been deprived of sleep. I needed a hot bath and a few hours' rest before dinner.

'I shall see you at dinner, I assume?'

'Yes, Dinu.'

'*Au revoir*, then.'

'*A bientôt.*'

Where could I hide the photograph of Răzvan? That was my first thought as I walked into the room I had been absent from all summer. Then I wondered if there was any reason why I should conceal it. He was the friend I had made in Paris, who had turned out to be the ideal companion and guide to the city for the uninformed and guileless Dinu Grigorescu. I had no cause to be secretive about this man in his late thirties, handsome as he was, captured smiling at the camera by a street photographer on the Champs-Elysées. No one was to know, unless I told them, that he was my deflowerer, my consummate and passionate lover, my precious Răzvănel.

I would have the snapshot enlarged and framed.

I slept. It was the sleep of death, with my mother at its centre.

'Welcome home,' she said, rising from her grave. 'It is good to have you back in the bosom of the family.'

'Mamă.'

'So you have remembered me, you forgetful boy?'

'Yes, Mamă.'

'Your thoughts are all of that wretched man who has stolen your heart. Where are your prayers for me? Where are my Dinu's tears?'

'I have been too busy living for myself. Forgive me, I beg of you.'

'You did not even stop to look at my portrait at the top

of the staircase. You walked straight past it. You have never been so circumspect before.'

'You are wrong, my darling mother. I saw your dark eyes and hair and the pearl choker and the blue silk gown you wore for the artist who painted you in 1908, the year you gave birth to me. Of course I stopped and looked at you.'

I heard what I said to her and believed it. There was no reason for me not to.

She laughed as she had never laughed in life. It was the cackle of a witch or a woman who had been painfully hurt and maligned. She did not sound remotely like Elena Grigorescu.

I told her she was frightening me. I screamed at her to stop.

I awoke to find my father at the foot of the bed.

'Are you emerging from a bad dream, Dinu?'

'Yes, Tată, I think I am.'

'Have you been eating an excess of cheese? Dr Stănescu is of the opinion that Brie and Camembert provoke the dormant imagination to the wildest of fantasies. You must be more careful with your diet.'

I promised him I would be more careful, now that I was away from the culinary temptations of Paris.

'You may dress casually for dinner, my son. No members of the royal family or government ministers will be present. It is going to be a modest affair.'

Then he was gone, with the name 'Elisabeta' on my lips, waiting to be voiced.

Ah, that 'modest affair'. My lawyer father had a sly way with words. There was nothing remotely modest about the event that was staged for my homecoming that late September evening in the dining room at Carmen Sylva 4. The encounter with Elisabeta should have alerted my dull brain to what was coming, but I was exhausted after the journey and thinking only, and selfishly, of Răzvan. It did not surprise me when I learned, later, that she had become my stepsister.

'I had hoped, Dinu, that I would have had the privilege of introducing you to Elisabeta's mother first, but it was not to be. Once she is in communion with her perfumes and soaps and lotions, it is difficult to extricate her. When she emerges, Dinu, you can rest assured that my new wife – your new mother – will smell like Helen of Troy or some such divine being.'

'Your new wife? My new mother?'

'Yes, Dinu. I married Amalia while you were living a luxurious *vie de Bohème* in Paris. You look taken aback, which is understandable, but are you not pleased for me?'

I could not, and would not, say I was. I observed, instead: 'I have not met her. I have no idea what kind of woman she is.'

'She is totally unlike our treasured Elena, Dinu, in every conceivable way. She has energy and wit and – this I know to my cost – a refined taste for beautiful clothes. The houses of Worth and Chanel would collapse without her custom.'

'Is she younger than you?'

'You asked that question disapprovingly. She is younger, yes, by five years.'

'Her husband, her first husband, is dead?'

'And her second.'

Before I could give expression to the consternation I felt, he said, with one of his rare smiles: 'She didn't murder them, if that is what is in your mind. This is the real world, Dinu, not some lurid novel.'

I had not considered that my still unseen stepmother might be a murderer, but the words 'lurid novel' gave me cause to wonder. I had never suspected the austere Cezar Grigorescu of being attracted to fiction, especially of the lurid kind.

'Ah, there she is, my darling Amalia.'

And there indeed she was, the Helen of Troy I hated on sight. Her every word, her every gesture, seemed intent on eradicating my mother's goodness and modesty.

'You are the prettiest boy in the world,' she declared. 'You are ravishing.'

'I am honoured to meet you,' I replied. 'My father has kept you a secret from me.'

'You must not blame me for the deception, Dinu. I pleaded with Cezar to be open and honest with you. Believe me, I did.'

'I believe you.'

She kissed me. I did not draw back in revulsion, much though I wanted to. The prettiest boy in the world – she had obviously travelled extensively – guessed on the instant that Amalia Grigorescu was a fabricator, a dealer in charm. I could be such a dealer too, I thought, as she led me by the hand into the dining-room my mother had graced throughout my childhood.

'You will tell me all about your Parisian adventures, won't you, Dinu?'

Yes, of course I will, Amalia, in abundant detail. I will reveal to you how, half-drunk and in a frenzy of lust, I made my unsteady way to Albert Le Cuziat's baths. I will inform you, with complete exactitude – for you would expect nothing less – how Honoré, soon to be identified as Răzvan, conquered the heart (the appropriate cliché of turgid fiction) of the pretty Romanian boy who had rechristened himself Jean-Pierre. I promise, Amalia, that you will be agog as I re-explore in words the explorations that Honoré and Jean-Pierre embarked upon that summer day, and how Răzvan and Dinu became sexual Marco Polos as their mutual desire refused to wane. All this, and more, I will pass on to you as we take tea or coffee in the delicate Grigorescu china that was my mother's pride, for it was she who designed it.

'You have turned very thoughtful, Dinu.'

'I was thinking of how I should address you.'

'Ah, that is problematical, isn't it? I am not your mother, and "stepmother" smacks too much of the Brothers Grimm's Fairy Tales. I am of the belief that we should be very, very modern and that you should call me Amalia, providing that you pronounce my name without the passionate emphasis your father, my utterly divine Cezar, puts on it.'

'That presents no difficulty, Amalia.'

There were four guests at table, each of them invited by my father to share his delight in Amalia's wit and beauty. I have forgotten them – a lack of recall I attribute to the fact that they never appeared at the house near Cişmigiu again. I do remember Amalia as a shining presence and that the Château Talbot we drank with the lamb Denisa had cooked in the slow-roasted Romanian tradition was of a sublime mellowness.

My dream-or-nightmare mother had told me the truth. Her portrait was no longer at the top of the central staircase. It had been replaced by a landscape painting of a view of fields in Transylvania over which a lone stork hovered.

Gheorghe handed me a letter with a Paris postmark. I laid it beside my breakfast plate and went on eating.

'May I have the stamps, Master Dinu, when you have finished with the envelope?'

'You may have them now. Are the Lindbergh stamps collectors' items?'

'They soon will be.'

There was a message from my lover inside, written on the flimsiest paper.

'Here you are, Gheorghe. I shall read this in my study.'

I slid the message into a pocket of my dressing-gown and went upstairs. I dreaded its contents, suspecting a farewell note that would have cost my practical, sensible lover great anguish to write. I shaved and bathed before I dared to look at it.

My dear friend – I miss your amusing company – Paris is the duller without you – You must send me the news of your homecoming, which I await with interest – I have plans to visit our country as soon as I can – I am still working at Les Deux Cygnes – How is your appetite? Mine is not healthy – I had a dream last night in which I was an EXPLORER, can you believe? – The autumn is almost over and I fear a cold and lonely winter – I send you my respectful greetings – R.P.

My loving correspondent, whose affection for his beloved Dinu I detected between the dashes, had penned these cryptic lines with my father and his prying servants in mind. There was some deciphering to do – the loss of appetite; the word EXPLORER used to dramatic effect; his fear of a 'cold and lonely winter'. Could Cezar Grigorescu, the keenest legal intelligence in Romania, see that 'appetite' was not confined to the need for food, that the boastful EXPLORER was not a Columbus or Marco Polo, and that R.P.'s fears of coldness and loneliness were different in quality from those he shared with thousands of others at the chilly close of every year?

I wrote Răzvan an immoderate, unguarded reply, which I

took to the Central Post Office. I had it registered, to ensure that my words of love and lust were not delivered elsewhere, or lost completely. They were meant to speed to him alone, with the accuracy of Diana's arrow.

'It seems that you weren't appreciative of the expensive parting gift I arranged for you in Paris.'

'Which expensive parting gift was that, Tată?'

'Your question is impudent, Dinu. There are not many young men who can afford to visit Mme Laurette's establishment. I gave you the precious opportunity to assert your manhood with a beautiful young woman of experience and charm. It was my best intention to spare you the bloody horrors of the virginal wedding-bed. Why didn't you fuck her?'

'I had no wish to.'

'Why was that? What was wrong with this Sonia?'

'There was nothing wrong with her. There was nothing wrong with her at all.'

'I am bewildered, Dinu.'

'I had no desire to go where others had gone before me,' I said, hearing the disgust in my voice. I continued: 'I could not rise to the occasion.'

My father smiled.

'It's an old joke, but a good one, Dinu. Shall we try the experiment again, here in Bucharest?'

'I should prefer that we didn't,' I said. 'Not yet.'

'As you wish. I am not pleased with the idea that you will go through life your mother's son.'

'What type of son is that?'

'A prig. A holier-than-thou plaster saint. A man who is almost too good to live.'

The word 'good' was apropos, for Elena Grigorescu

believed in the healing powers of goodness, as she often counselled me. But she was averse to priggishness, to moral superiority in any form, as my blinkered father ought to have been aware.

'Believe me, Tată, I am not too good. I very much want to live a moderately wicked life.'

'Moderately wicked?' What was I saying? I did not consider my love for Răzvan wicked, whatever the world thought. That world, I understood, included Cezar Grigorescu. Perhaps I was 'moderately wicked' in the ways most people are – obsessed with themselves and their own needs; intolerant and envious; thoughtless and inconsiderate in their dealings with others. These were some of the everyday sins my mother had warned me not to commit.

'I hope and trust, Dinu, that you are not set upon disappointing me totally.'

I assured him, as best I could, that he would be proud of me one day. It was my devoutest wish.

We embraced, after a manly fashion, and I was struck, I recall, by the smell of his sickly-sweet cologne. Did it captivate Amalia as much as it nauseated me?

Oh, what madness, I thought happily, as I placed the enlarged and framed snapshot of my beloved on the bedside table. I could see him now as soon as I awoke and before I drifted into sleep. He was there beside me at all hours.

I had left the door of my room open. Amalia entered, apologizing for intruding on my privacy.

'Who is that wild-looking creature, Dinu?'

'He is a friend I made in Paris. He is Romanian. His name is Răzvan Popescu.'

'But he's the prince's boy.'

'Yes, he is, or was. The prince died in England some time ago.'

'Are you very close to him, my impossibly beautiful stepson?'

I considered my impossible beauty before answering. 'Yes, I am. I am, Amalia.'

'I should like, in the finest tradition of Romanian decadence, to seduce you, Dinu. To take a stepson in adultery is so exquisitely decadent. May I tempt you?'

'In God's name, no.'

'You look terrified by my little joke. Has the ogress frightened you?'

'No, of course not,' I lied.

'I promise you, in return for a kiss on the cheek, that I shall keep your secret safe from Cezar. You could make it easier for me by hiding the prince's boy's photograph somewhere – in a drawer, perhaps, to which only you have the key.'

'But why?'

'Cezar would recognize your close friend instantly. He was, and still is, the subject of gossip in Parisian society and here in Bucharest. The prince has made the simple peasant notorious, if not famous.'

'Răzvan is not simple. He is an intelligent man. He speaks flawless French.'

'My dear Dinu, you must endeavour not to be too unhappy. Are you in contact with him?'

Was she, I wondered, my father's spy, feigning concern for me?

'No,' I lied again. 'I am still awaiting a reply to a letter I wrote him a month ago.'

'I trust that he is being discreet, rather than cruel.'

'You can trust in his discretion.'

She said: 'I most sincerely hope so' and, enfolding my hand in hers, she went on: 'You are resentful of my place in Cezar's affections. I understand your resentment. I am not cast in your mother's mould, Dinu, my dear one. I am a slut by comparison. I cannot believe in her God. And yours.'

'And mine, yes.'

'He has not been kind to us. He seems, from my reading of the Bible, to be exceedingly bad-tempered and quick – all too quick – to take offence. But if He offers you consolation, then so be it.'

'He does.'

'I don't think that He, even He, is capable of protecting you from Cezar's anger and disappointment if your earthly father sees this photograph. Do be careful, Dinu.'

I thanked her for the warning.

'I am very serious. You are such an innocent, for all your sophisticated cleverness. Can't you understand, my sweet one, that your behaviour is – what is the precise word I am seeking? – perverse?'

'I do understand, and I really don't think I care.'

'Then you should care – for your safety; for your dignity; for your future.'

'What do *you* care?' I asked her, unaware in that moment of my cruelty.

'Oh, I should say, in my role as the wicked, or perhaps, downright evil stepmother, that I don't give a damn about you. But I am not that figure of popular, vulgar imagination. How could I not be concerned for you, Dinu? Your very eyes crave affection. Yes, they are looking beyond me, even as I talk to you. They are looking at your Răzvan Popescu.'

'You are being fanciful, Amalia.'

'Ah, you called me Amalia, and without that cynical

edge to your voice I have become accustomed to. We are progressing. We are progressing faster than I had hoped.'

'What do you mean?'

'I mean that I know something important about you that Cezar will refuse to acknowledge. You are irretrievably – not to say, irresponsibly – in love with the prince's boy. You are, aren't you?'

'Yes, I am.'

'I will keep your secret safe from Cezar for as long as I can. I will keep it safe from Bucharest society as well. You can put your trust in me, Dinu.'

In that moment I had no reason to doubt her. I feared that she was becoming my closest confidante, even – and this was a greater fear – my most intimate friend.

I wrote constantly to Răzvan from the country whose king was eight years old. I received cryptic postcards in reply. It was rainy in Paris or it was sunny. R wished that D was there. He said nothing that would make my father suspicious, though Amalia and her already worldly daughter understood the precise nature of his wish. I was the prince's boy's pining lover, contenting himself with sepia views of the Eiffel Tower, the Arc de Triomphe and the Tuileries.

Then, one day in the summer of 1929, Gheorghe brought me a substantial letter with a Parisian postmark. I gave him the eight or so stamps for his collection before I had the courage to read the contents of the envelope.

Honoured Sir, it began:

My dear Silviu (perhaps) or Alexandru (perhaps) or Dinu (most certainly), I am writing to you in the capacity of a concerned friend – a term I seldom, if ever, employ. If you are planning, with or without your father's money and permission, to return to Paris, I should alert you to the distressing fact that life here is unsettled. I fear I shall have to close the doors of my Temple of Immodesty sooner than I could have anticipated. You were a welcome guest there, Domnule Grigorescu, for a day or two, as I am certain you will remember. Business – to employ that distasteful bourgeois word – is not flourishing.

There are two persons responsible for my temporary fall from immoral grace. The first is that Russian scoundrel Safarov, who has forsworn his formidable sadistic talents in favour of a quiet life in the tender arms of a wealthy vintner's widow in Bordeaux. The other offender is Safarov's once-ecstatic victim, who threatened to withdraw his custom unless I provided him with a replacement brute. I scoured the docks for three wearisome nights before I chanced upon a beast from faraway Brazil with a scant command of the French language, although his brown eyes brightened as soon as I mentioned L'ARGENT. *He was born with a* PECTUS EXCA-VATUM *(a sunken chest) but he is otherwise statuesque. His torso is festooned with inexplicable tattoos, apart from the inevitable heart pierced by the mischievous Cupid. He also boasts a strange blue and red sign above his groin which resembles a feather (a macaw's, perhaps) and a pair of crossed keys and a miniature crucifixion on his left arm. He is due to molest the industrialist this forthcoming Wednesday. I can but hope that Louis, as we have decided to call him, will be Safarov's repellently worthy successor.*

Allow me to turn to the subject of Honoré or Răzvan – have I put the accent in its rightful place? – of whom, I feel certain, you wish to hear. Of course you do. Prince E's boy is often excessively drunk on the coarsest red wine, if his breath is any indication. We meet rarely and accidentally and our conversations begin with social banalities and end with his lamenting the absence of the enticing Romanian who broke his heart. He informs me that he sends you postcards in code because he is terrified that your forbidding Papa will smell a rat, to resort to a cliché that cannot fail to summon up a haunting vision of my cherished friend M. Proust. I have ceased to offer him employment. His apartment was paid for years ago by the prince and he assures me that he earns enough as a barman to satisfy his daily needs, which do not include – he is adamant on this matter – sexual gratification. I believe him, alas.

I trust you are well, as I am not. The House of Impudence is taking its toll on my nerves and sanity.

Salutations,
Albert Le Cuziat

I hid the letter, along with Răzvan's snapshot and the cryptic postcards, in a volume of Eminescu's poems the lawyer who owned Carmen Sylva 4 never consulted. They were in the melancholy company of distant horns and ominous alders and thoughts of death.

I was arguing with my mother now. She had become the Elena I no longer wept for, but rather a religious tyrant, constantly accusing me of being faithless. Whenever I spoke of my deep and abiding love for Răzvan she did not hesitate to chastise me. Hell was my certain destination. If she had lived, she shouted, she would have protected me from such a dissolute specimen of humankind.

I almost replied that I was glad she hadn't lived. I should not have known ecstasy otherwise. But the hateful words did not make the journey from my heart to my tongue.

'You are not the son I left behind.'

I replied that I had glimpsed a fraction of the world, the world her church would have me ignore. I needed to function in that world, to explore its mysteries and contradictions.

I wanted to be a man of my own making. I wanted, in the autumn of 1929, to be in Răzvan's arms. Nowhere else in the entire universe remotely appealed to me. It was my earthly idea of heaven.

My once-compassionate mother chuckled at this revelation. I pleaded with her to stop, but she carried away with her mocking laughter. I was abject now, where before I had been adoring and trusting.

'Oh, Mamă, Mamă, I cannot help myself.'

'Yes, you can. Take confession and cleanse the mind and the body you have sullied.'

That sullied body, in a lonely bed at four in the morning, was in a frenzied state, longing for the man who had sullied it to appear miraculously in his hirsute splendour and sully it further.

I wrote to Răzvan telling him I was employed as Reader in French Literature at the university, having achieved my doctorate after more than two years of intense and dedicated study. I was earning a living of sorts. I was a man with a monthly salary, however meagre, and no longer entirely dependent on my absurdly wealthy father.

This was in 1930, almost three years to the day when we had last kissed, last embraced.

The predictable postcard, a sepia reproduction of the *Mona Lisa*, arrived in December.

My good friend D, I have heard that my mother is sick. She lives in Corcova in your country. I shall be leaving Paris soon to be with her. I expect I shall be with her and my family for some time. There must be a town or city other than Bucharest where we can renew our interesting friendship. R.

Our interesting friendship? My blood raced as I read those words. Răzvan was getting nearer to me, I realized. He would soon be only a train journey away from the Reader in French Literature I knew, or hoped I knew, he still loved.

'What is my son wearing today, Amalia?'
  'I believe it is called a suit, Cezar.'
  'I can see that it is a suit. What is the material?'
  'Velvet, my love.'
  'Should a man wear velvet?'
  'I think this man should, yes.'
  'He used to dress plainly and sensibly before you decided to make a dandy of him.'
  'What are you complaining about? Dinu was born to wear gorgeous clothes. Some men are.'
  'He is making himself too conspicuous.'
  'Why should he not be conspicuous?'
  'Because he is not on a stage cavorting before an audience. He is walking along the boulevards of Bucharest.'

This conversation, or versions of it, took place regularly in my rebellious years from 1929 to 1934. The word 'depraved' was applied to me by some of my staid colleagues, though a few of them were envious of my freedom from convention. Others despised me covertly, as seems to be the custom in our beleaguered country.

Yet I was pretending to be carefree. During those five years I saw Răzvan twice, and on both occasions I forswore the fancy clothing Amalia and Elisabeta had chosen for me. I went to him unadorned, in the same kind of plain cotton shirts and light woollen trousers he remembered me wearing in Paris. I was his Dinuleț, he my Răzvănel. We were reunited first in the smallest of small hotels in Eforie, on the

Black Sea, not far from Constanţa, where Ovid, banished from Rome, had lived in exile. My father was pleased that I had discarded velvet and silk and cashmere for my coastal holiday, since it meant that his son and heir would not bring disgrace on the honourable name of Grigorescu.

Răzvan's revered Angela had died, and there was to be no work for him on the estate. The prince's brother found his presence embarrassing and suggested that he return to Paris, the most liberated and welcoming city in all of Europe. It was kindly said. Prince A understood that Răzvan was no longer a boy in want of an education, but a sophisticated middle-aged man who was a stranger even to Bogdan, Mircea and Irina, despite their mutual loss. Corcova was no longer his home, as it had promised to be for ever when he was an inquisitive child. He had held Angela's cold hands, kissed her cold cheeks, closed down the cold shutters that had been her eyelids while his brothers and sister wept in the shadows. He had no further cause to stay.

He was reluctant to leave Romania immediately. There were so many towns and cities and villages he had never visited. He telephoned the Grigorescu household one evening in June 1932. He told Gheorghe that he wished to speak to the teacher of French, whose name he had temporarily forgotten. Was he, by chance, at home?

He was. He wanted to shed tears of joy on hearing the captivating voice, made the more wondrous because of the hissing and crackling sounds that were its heaven-sent accompaniment.

'Dinicu? Dinuleţ?'

'Is that Răzvănel?' I whispered, out of Gheorghe's earshot.

'It is. I have come back to claim you.'

'Are you sure?'

'Yes, I am. You are not my Dinicu if you think otherwise.'

'I have to see you. I must see you.'

'You will, my sweet. You will, very soon. Do you think you could persuade your forbidding father to let you take a vacation by the Black Sea? You must be alone, if that is possible.'

'I shall try.'

'Try hard. I shall be in Constanţa in two weeks. I have much to tell you. I will telephone you again, I promise.'

It was a promise he kept, as I prayed he would. Elena interrupted my prayers with the caution that I was praying to the devil, not the God she had taught me to worship. The devil in the flesh had me in his grasp. If I wasn't careful, I would be beyond forgiveness.

My father was quite content for me to have a seaside holiday. There was but one proviso, once I had assured him I would dress normally, and that was that I should spend more time in the sun. I was still, in his opinion, unnaturally pale.

I told him I would persevere in my efforts to come back to Bucharest as brown as a berry.

Amalia and Elisabeta were suspicious on the instant when I observed, sheepishly, that I was going to Constanţa by myself.

'Does my naughty stepson have an assignation?'

'No, he doesn't.'

'You will need special clothes for the beach. I shall arrange a fitting with my dear Leon Becker.'

'There is no need, Amalia, Elisabeta. I intend to dress plainly, for once, as I did when I was in Paris.'

They looked at each other and smiled. No more was said, since they were already party to the conspiracy. Răzvan wasn't mentioned, because there was no reason to mention him. The light in my eyes was evidence enough.

He telephoned again on the nineteenth of June. It was Denisa who picked up the receiver.

'Domnule Dinu, there is a man with a very hoarse voice wishing to speak to you.'

That hoarse voice lost its hoarseness when I asked, cautiously, 'Is that Răzvan?'

'It is, it is, it is. Will I be seeing my precious Dinicu soon?'

'Tomorrow? The day after? The day after that?'

'The day after, my sweet. I will be waiting for you on the station. I shall expect you late in the evening.'

Oh, it was a cumbersome journey, because the train stopped at every country station. I had no eye for the passing scenery or ears for my fellow travellers, who came and went with their packages and briefcases and luggage. I ceased to be observant for hours on end. I had only the Răzvan captured in the precious photograph in mind. I could not sleep and I could not read the novel by Raymond Radiguet which I opened and closed a dozen or more times. I was elated at the prospect of being reunited with him and downcast at the thought that he might not recognize the boy he had loved so intensely five years earlier in Paris. I was twenty-four now, he forty-three. I feared his disappointment, his tactful rejection of the Dinu he called Dinicu and Dinuleţ. I could not bear the idea of going back to Bucharest without his warming presence in my future.

There was a moment, a chilling moment, on the platform in Constanţa, when I wondered if he had really phoned me, really invited me to join him by the Black Sea. Perhaps I had imagined the phone calls, the postcards, in my demented longing for him. Where, where on God's earth, was he?

He was standing by the barrier, his arms outstretched as I approached him. He was there before me. It was the shape of him I saw first, then his dark beard, then his slightly receding hair. I was suddenly in a haze of happiness. I had nothing to say to him, yet, for the words I had been saying to him for five years – the terms of endearment I had been whispering to him in my bedroom; in my study at the university; in bars and restaurants – had vanished from my tongue. I was silent and so was he. The barrier no longer between us, we embraced. The smell of him was in my nostrils again, that comforting and consoling odour that was peculiar to him and him alone. I basked in it. I breathed it in – deeply, contentedly.

'We must go, Dinicu. It is late. There is a horse and carriage waiting for us. I am taking you to Eforie. It is a quiet spot. We will be happy there.'

I heard Răzvan tell the driver that the son he had not seen for five years, thanks to his estranged wife's possessiveness, was here beside him. They would be taking a short holiday together.

He was my father when we checked into the hotel, with its view of the beach. There were other guests on the terrace, already drunk, whom we joined for a celebratory glass or two of sparkling wine. I was introduced as Dinu Popescu, a name I was strangely happy to possess.

We retired – that was the word Răzvan used – to our room. The drunks, who seemed determined to get drunker, bade Domnule Popescu and his son goodnight.

Our Popescu suite was Spartan, with little decoration to delight the eye. We were pretenders once more, as Honoré and Jean-Pierre had been, with me deprived of my rightful name. My pretend father kissed me and ruffled my hair and slowly and carefully undressed me, folding my shirt and vest and trousers neatly and placing them with untypical tidiness on a chair. He appeared to be beyond passion in his sweet attentiveness. His elaborate carefulness excited me to near-distraction, as he intended it should, and I shivered as he removed my underpants and socks.

'You have not lost your beauty for me.'

'Please may I take my Tată's clothes off?'

'You may, my incestuous son.'

I showed no care, no slow consideration, in my longing to have him naked before me. I was desperate to be explored and as desperate to travel around the man whose body I worshipped. I let his clothes, his protective armour, fall in a heap to the floor.

'This is a hotel, Dinicu. We must be very discreet. I will strangle you, I promise, if you scream or moan.'

I neither screamed nor moaned, though I think I made a noise much like purring as our love-making progressed.

'Răzvănel.'

'I am older and plumper, aren't I?'

'If you are, it does not matter. It does not matter at all.'

'You may think differently in the cold light of morning.'

'Be silent, Tată. Mon père. My daddy.'

We slept, entwined. Then we separated, before dawn, and resumed our geographical studies, in silence. Long absence had made my heart grow fonder. It was overflowing with affection now.

'We cannot stay in bed all day, my dearest. The human race is composed of suspicious people. We must be innocents while we are here. I am your proud father and you are my doting offspring. We have to be actors in Eforie.'

I vowed that I would learn my lines and never stray

from them. I intended to be word-perfect. The role of Dinu Popescu was one I wished to play to absolute perfection.

We strolled along the shore after breakfast, stopping to embrace when there was no one else in sight. We spoke, when the need was on us, in French.

'If I had not been the prince's boy, his adopted son, I would never have met you, Dinu,' he said as we sat down to dinner that evening. 'It might have been better for the two of us if he hadn't educated me.'

'If, if, if – what are you saying to me, Răzvan?'

'I hardly know. I am drowning in confusion. I have no family now that my mother is dead. Bogdan, Irina and Mircea are like strangers to me, although I still love them. I might have lived in Corcova all my days. There are worse things than being a simple peasant, toiling in the fields from sunrise to sunset. Oh, far, far worse.'

'What shall we have to eat, Tată?' I asked loudly as a waiter approached our table.

'Fish, *mon fils*. You do not come to the Black Sea to eat anything else.'

So we ate grilled carp, and summer fruits, and ice cream, accompanied by more wine than I had drunk in ages. It was cheap stuff that the prince and Cezar Grigorescu would have scorned to offer their guests. I drank it because he was drinking it. I smiled at the notion of its being our love potion, or perhaps my poisoned chalice.

'You are teaching your son bad habits,' said a woman who had been looking appreciatively at my father – yes, he had to be that – for most of the evening. 'I am being facetious, dear sir. You make a handsome pair.'

He rose and kissed her hand, as Romanian gentlemen do.

She simpered and wished us the sleep of the just, if not the wicked. She waved to us from the door of the dining room.

'Silly cow.'

'She desires you, my lovely Tată. You could be hers without even asking.'

'I suppose I still possess a certain allure.'

'You do. I want you now.'

'Not here in the restaurant?'

'Anywhere will please me, but may I suggest that room number 9 is more appropriate?'

And so, in room 9, we clung to one another, and that was all we did until daybreak. He slept and snored and farted with his arms around me while I lay awake. I kissed his fingertips and nestled into him and tried not to imagine the immediate future, when we would again be separated. I was to be his, completely his, in the morning, and for the moment nothing else concerned, or mattered to, me.

I was asleep, in fact, when he claimed me. I was dreaming of him before the dream became an event in the real world.

Yes, he was right to say he looked older and that he was plumper. He had flesh to clutch that had not been clutchable in Paris. His face was rounder and redder too. These changes to his body were of no consequence to his adoring Dinicu, as I had to reassure him on more occasions than I can remember.

'You are vain, Răzvănel.'

'Am I? I suppose I am. But not as vain as the prince.'

'You showed me photographs of him. He was handsome.'

'He was.'

'You never told me that he killed himself.'

'Are you sure? In that case, how do you know?'

'I heard about it from M. Le Cuziat, over an expensive luncheon at the Ritz.'

'Which you paid for, I recollect.'

'Your recollection is completely accurate,' I remarked with deliberate and, I hoped, diverting pomposity.

'And what did the monster reveal?'

'That his suicide took place in an English hotel and that he considered the prince a coward.'

Several minutes, what seemed like an hour of several minutes, passed before he responded.

'The prince, my benefactor, had suffered a stroke. Was that one of the gossipy Albert's revelations?'

'I don't recall that it was.'

The prince, Răzvan said, had travelled, in the company of friends, to Japan, the land of the chrysanthemum, the flower most favoured by all sophisticated Parisians. Somewhere between Tokyo and Paris, the left side of his face had frozen stiff. It had become totally immobile. What was the cause? There was speculation that the prince had contracted syphilis, but no one knew where, or from whom.

'My benefactor was always elegant. His preferred colour was blue. In the remaining months of his life, he covered up his shame – for that is what he called it – with a blue scarf. I still have it, Dinicu. He wanted me to have it. I do not understand why.'

I did not understand either.

'Perhaps it will be my turn to cover my face with it one day.'

'Why should you do that?'

'When I no longer want the world to look at me.'

'Why should you want that?'

'Oh, Dinu,' he suddenly exploded. 'I am wretched beyond words.'

'You are drunk,' I observed calmly, with no hint of

accusation. 'You are drunk, my sweetheart. It's the grape talking, not Răzvănel. I am here with you. You should be happy that I am here with you.'

'Should I be? Who says I should?'

'I do. I say it emphatically,' I said without emphasis. 'I say you should.'

He glared at me for a few terrifying minutes. I held his stare with the nearest thing to a smile that I could manage. I waited, with feigned patience, for my lover to be returned to me. When he came back, it was with a long sigh. He begged my forgiveness, which I granted him on the instant.

Răzvan laughed when I told him that both my denigrators and my small number of admirers in Bucharest regarded me as a *bonjouriste* because of my predilection for speaking French whenever I had the opportunity.

'That's what the prince called me, too, but as a joke.'

It wasn't a joke anymore, in 1932, and would become an insult of the worst kind as the decade progressed. To be a dandyish *bonjouriste* meant that you favoured Paris rather than Berlin, the unlikely Mecca that attracted a new breed of pilgrims.

'"I have made the peasant boy a *bonjouriste* and I am very proud of my achievement" is what the prince said.'

My lover's suitcase contained not only clothes and toiletries but tattered, much read, books as well. Creangă and Eminescu were there with Baudelaire and Maupassant and the final volumes of Proust, in which our mutual acquaintance, in the guise of Jupien, appears in all his mischievous splendour. Few Pandars have been immortalized while they were still living. It would be Albert Le Cuziat's privilege to remain as constant a presence as Vautrin or Rastignac, those somewhat more beguiling literary villains. He would never now be completely anonymous, like the majority of the human race.

I began to understand, as the almost blissful days went by, that Răzvan had no resting place. He had been expelled, or banished, from Corcova and he was lonely in Paris since few of the prince's friends wanted to spend time in the company of somebody they considered glum. Was I to be his saviour, his refuge? I dared to hope so. I dared to hope beyond hope that his promise that we would be together for the rest of our lives might become reality.

I was determined to find out more about his past than he had granted me in our previous, quickly curtailed conversations. I needed to be subtle and tactful. I had to catch him in the relative calm before a drunken storm. I loathed to tell myself that I was beginning to be afraid of him.

It was in just such a state of calm that I asked him why he had chosen to work for Albert Le Cuziat.

'I have been waiting for that question, ever since we gave ourselves to each other five years ago.'

'And now I am waiting for your answer.'

'You will be granted it, rest assured. I will give it to you slowly and carefully, for it demands unclouded thought.'

It was early in the day. He was drinking Turkish coffee. I saw him again in the doorway of his cubicle, smiling on the stumbling boy who would soon reveal his identity, as he would his. It had been, for me, the prologue to enchantment. I wondered, for the briefest of moments, if I was still enchanted by him, and just as briefly I decided I was.

'Did I work for M. Albert?' he asked himself. 'I honoured his House of Mischief – oh, he has a hundred names for the place – with my baleful presence, but I cannot say, with my hand on my heart, a cliché the prince would have deplored, that I actually worked for him. No, no, Dinicu – there are two kinds of work that I recognize. One is the work of the body and the other is that of the mind. My forefathers, my father and mother, my sister and brothers have all toiled for a living, but I have an intelligence denied to them. It was the prince's gift to me. Did I say gift? Curse, perhaps. My work of the mind was learning French, studying the architecture of Chartres – the prince's church par excellence – and reading the books, looking at the paintings and listening to the music that met with his discerning approval. Are you impressed by my erudite use of language?'

I said I was.

'That is about all I have left.'

'Răzvănel, please answer my question.'

'Be patient. I will answer it.'

I waited for him to speak again.

'You are the only client – I hate to use that word – I ever made love to.'

'Is that the truth?'

'Why should it not be? The prince had been dead a few years when Le Cuziat invited me to become one of his "purveyors of naughtiness". That is another of his many fancy phrases, his "curlicues". I accepted his offer, but on my own carefully considered terms. I was to be untouchable. I would show his aristocrats – some of them rich, most of them married – what they wanted to see of the prince's boy's body, but there was to be nothing beyond that. They could feast their eyes on me and that was all. I was indifferent to their displays of affection, their promise to buy me the jewels and trinkets of which I had no need. I became adept at sneering. If they dared to put a hand on me, I reprimanded them for being so brazen. They were breaking my rules. Oh, Dinicu, I had to endure much sobbing and whimpering and accusations of being callous, but I think – indeed, I know – that they enjoyed themselves. If there is such a place as a seventh heaven, they were occupying it when they were with me. They knew who I was – the surrogate son of a cultivated prince – and that knowledge excited them almost to a frenzy. Until I met you, I was a brilliant actor.'

'You aren't any more?'

It was the silliest, the most heartless, question of my life. He looked wounded by it. He *was* wounded by it.

'I am so sorry, Răzvan. You have never acted for my benefit. You have always been sincere with me.'

He averted his gaze, preferring to smile at the 'silly cow' who had flirted with him.

'Oh please, Răzvănel. Please, my darling. Please forgive my stupidity.'

He turned back to me. He shook his head. He sighed.

'I am acting now for you, for the only time. I am pretending to be offended. And now the pretence is over. Your father is impossibly in love with his fragile son. Impossibly, impossibly. Room 9 beckons. Let us not waste another second getting there. Come on.'

I am tempted to weep now at the grace he bestowed upon me that day. We went to room 9 and transported its confines, as the English poet John Donne says, into an everywhere.

There are times when kisses are much more persuasive, and adequate, than words.

When the 'silly cow' came to our table and asked if she could buy us a bottle of champagne, Răzvan replied that we would be honoured to drink it with her.

Her name was Luiza, she told us as she sat down. She had been newly widowed. She was here to enjoy the sea air. We were quite the handsomest father and son she had ever seen. She had not embarrassed us, had she? Before we could reply, she continued by commenting on my exquisite pallor and his suntanned attractiveness. Răzvan was delighted to see that she was already emboldened by drink.

'You have such strong hands, Domnule Popescu,' she said, stroking one of them.

'My son's are prettier. His fingers are very finely tapered. They are much prized by me.'

I wondered if she understood exactly what he was implying, but she seemed not to. I hoped he would stop teasing her.

'Where is your wife and young Dinu's mother?'

'She's dead, like your husband. Her passing was an enormous loss to us.'

'I can believe that.'

Oh, you silliest of silly drunken cows, I thought, hearing her expressing commiseration. We have different mothers, I wanted to say – the Elena who was still chastising me; the Angela whose Răzvan had perplexed and maybe even frightened her. Our enormous losses were subtly diverse. I was beginning to hope the champagne would run dry and the evening come to an end.

Then she fell instantly, and startlingly, asleep, as if some Puck or Ariel had dropped a magic potion into her eyes. We left her. We drifted quietly away. We talked of my exquisite pallor and his suntanned attractiveness as we climbed the flight of stairs that led us to room 9, our drab and unimaginatively decorated paradise.

His exceptionally strong hands and my finely tapered fingers were soon conjoined, and the night passed, as I recall, blissfully.

*

There was a thunderstorm the following day.

'It might be the end of the world, Dinicu. This isn't ordinary rain, it's a monsoon.'

I found the sight and sound of it exhilarating. I swear the sky turned green with every bolt of thunder and flash of lightning. I felt insignificant, happily so, as the sea boiled over and the trees swayed.

Răzvan had hidden himself under the bed.

'What are you doing there?'

'I am terrified. I always have been,' he whimpered.

'Why?'

He was too frightened to answer. He was huddled up like a foetus.

I opened the windows and went out on to the balcony, enjoying the near-warmth of the raindrops that fell on the lover of the abject coward inside.

'It's getting closer. It is getting much closer.'

'What is?'

'The lightning.'

'You are talking nonsense. The storm is abating. You are being very childish.'

He emerged from his hiding place two hours later, when something close to tranquillity had been restored.

'I need a very strong drink – a brandy or a whisky.'

I went down to the bar and returned with a triple measure of cognac – enough, I reasoned, to calm every one of his shattered nerves.

'I saw someone struck by lightning, Dinu, when I was a very little boy in Corcova. She was a pregnant woman, so two lives were incinerated – is that the word? – at once. She was set afire. She was standing under a tree, to protect herself, but she wasn't spared. I see her whenever there's a storm.'

I held him to me. I was the comforter now. I was his protector, his mother and father, for many precious moments. He said he was sorry that I should see him so wretched.

I realized that I loved him in his cowardly state. He had become a Răzvan hitherto unknown to me, a man more fragile than I had ever suspected.

Răzvan said he would accompany me to Bucharest and take another train on to Paris. He had seen enough of Romania. Everyone, with the delicious exception of his Dinicu, irritated or bored him. He then revealed that he was in the mood to write a memoir. He was thinking of calling it *The Prince's Boy*, for that was who he was. His real father was the mystery of mysteries, a man whose gentleness had been denied him by unanticipated death. It was Prince E who had moulded and created the clever individual he was today. It was Prince E who should be praised, or blamed, for Răzvan Popescu's present condition.

'Have I the will to do it, Dinicu? Have I the determination?'

'Of course you have,' I answered, extracting even the tiniest hint of doubt from my voice.

The letter I read that morning, while Răzvan was taking a last swim in the Black Sea, is in my possession now. The paper has yellowed, the purple ink has faded, but to my inner eye it looks the same as when I opened it in the summer of 1932. He had asked me to pack his valise in a tidy fashion, since he was embarking on a long journey. His sophistication did not extend to the neat arrangement of clothes and toiletries, of books and personal mementoes, in a suitcase.

It fell out of his copy of *Une Vie*. The envelope had a London postmark. I opened it cautiously, fearful of its contents. I felt guilty at reading what the prince had written to his protégé in 1919, a few days before he took his life, I surmised.

My Dear Răzvan,

It is my sincere wish that you prosper. Continue your studies. The Paris apartment is yours for life. There is money in the bank at your disposal for the future. Spend it responsibly to better yourself.

You will have noted how despondent I have been since my return from Japan. The mirror offers me no solace because the face that is reflected horrifies its once proud owner. I am not so much ugly as grotesque. I have the twisted expression of a freak in a chamber of horrors. I am repelled by what I see.

'I have of late, but wherefore I know not, lost all my mirth,' as Hamlet says. I am the 'quintessence of dust', nothing more. Remember me without rancour if you can.

E.B.

I placed the letter back inside the book and said nothing of it to Răzvan when he returned to Room 9. It would soon be time to leave Eforie. We were still father and son as we sat on the bus that took us to Constanța.

We found ourselves a table in the salon at the Gara de Nord. We had another hour and a half together before the train that would terminate in Paris was due to depart.

'You could come with me, Dinicu. You could come and live with me.'

'Not yet, my love. Not just yet.'

I had explained to him during our stay in Eforie why I had to remain, without him, in Bucharest. I had commitments to honour. I was a respected teacher and a moderately successful journalist, reviewing books and plays for moderately liberal magazines and newspapers. I hoped, in time, to be financially independent.

'There are outlets for your cleverness in Paris, Dinicu. There are plenty of them. I will pay for your ticket.'

'No, no. I can't go with you to Paris. I want to. You must never doubt that I want to. Please send me letters from now on, Răzvănel, instead of those bland postcards.'

'I shall be lonely.'

'So shall I.'

The truth was, and is, that I feared to be with him. I sensed that the time had come for us to hurt each other. A few more weeks or months apart might be beneficial to both of us, absurd though it seemed. Besides, I craved his respect. I was beginning to be too old and cynical now to have him think of me solely as his beautiful boy. Hadn't we progressed beyond attractiveness, enchanting as it was? I said none of this as I looked at him, as I would always look at him, with adoration.

'Trust me, Răzvan. We shall be reunited for ever, I promise you.'

He raised his glass and smiled. 'If you say so.'

'I do.'

There are occasions when even the most sophisticated lovers indulge themselves by sounding like the vapid characters in a cheap romantic novel, of the kind consumed by lovelorn schoolgirls and regretful old maids. That is how we sounded now.

'There is a man at the bar who is staring at us.'

I turned and saw one of the clerks in my father's practice. I nodded by way of recognition and he did the same.

'He is a novice lawyer, much prized by Cezar Grigorescu.'

'He seems to be sneering.'

'That is his permanent expression. I think he was born with it. He will find it useful in the courtroom when he is acting on behalf of the prosecution.'

'He is studying my reflection in the mirror. Perhaps he considers me a criminal.'

'If he does, he is seriously misguided. Răzvan, I will join you in Paris as soon as possible, I swear to you. Let us be patient a little longer.'

'Patient? Longer? We have been separated for five years.'

'Yes,' was all I could manage to say.

'You have not asked me how many lovers I have clutched to my hairy bosom.'

'No, I haven't.'

'Then ask me now.'

I hesitated before asking him to let me know how many lovers he had clutched to his hairy bosom.

'As it happens—'

'As it happens?'

'As it happens, none. Not one. I have been conducting an affair with your image and my right hand. Until two weeks ago, that is.'

'So have I, Răzvănel. I mean *your* image and *my* right hand.'

We kissed one another's right hands. It was a kiss that transcended formality. It wasn't the kiss Romanians bestow on ladies they intend to seduce. It was the kiss – for both of us, then; for me, today – that specifically defined our love.

We said what we hoped would be a temporary farewell on platform 4. I was weeping and so was he. We Romanians cry easily. It is our national gift, to weep for our sorrows.

'You are my everlasting sweetheart,' he whispered.

*

My cousin Eduard dined with us the following evening. He had severed his business links with London and Paris and was now in residence again in Bucharest. He was to act as broker for the rejuvenated National Bank, which the previous year had forced the Marmorosch, Blank & Co. bank, a predominantly Jewish concern, into liquidation. Under its governor, Mihail Manoilescu, a man Eduard Vasiliu was proud to be personally acquainted with, the bank's intention was to represent the interests, and protect the interest, of its Christian customers. The Jews had held sway over the nation's money for too long.

I had never heard such talk at the Grigorescu family's table before. Cezar's criticism of politicians, his fellow lawyers and men in high office had contained no references to Jews. The word 'Jewish' had not been employed, in my presence, as a term of abuse. Yet here he was endorsing Eduard's opinion that the Hebraic fraternity had been a pernicious influence on Romanian affairs.

'I hope you are not including my heavenly Jewish dressmaker Leon Becker in your pernicious Hebraic fraternity, Eduard,' said Amalia. 'I should be helpless without him. Since Cezar restricted my clothes allowance to a shadow of what it was when he married me, Leon has copied the designs of Worth and Chanel on my instructions at a mere fraction of the Parisian price. Do you wish me to look dowdy – Eduard? Cezar? Dowdiness is not my métier.'

'Your humble Domnul Becker is neither a financier nor a politician, my love.'

After dinner, when Amalia and Elisabeta had left the gentlemen to drink cognac and smoke cigars, my father remarked casually that I had been spotted saying an emotional farewell to a middle-aged man at Gara de Nord.

'Is he the Popescu to whom you introduced me in Paris, Dinu?'

I looked at my cousin in silence for long minutes. 'Yes, he is,' I replied. 'The very same.'

'He is, I believe, the peasant boy Prince E adopted some thirty years ago.'

'Your belief is well-founded.'

'What is the nature of your friendship, my son?'

'I am confused by your question, Tată. Răzvan and I are friends, that is all.'

'Is that all?'

'Yes. We are soul mates.'

'Soul mates?'

'Soul mates. We love the same books, the same art, the same music, the same language.'

'You must find yourself a wife, Dinu. There is already speculation about you.'

'Speculation?'

'I fear so.'

'Of what kind?'

'It was your refusal to enjoy yourself at Mme Laurette's that alarmed us,' observed my increasingly uncousinly cousin. 'It seemed strange behaviour for a hot-blooded youth.'

'I was not attracted to Sonia.'

'You remember her name?'

'I cannot forget it.'

'There is a psychiatrist on Victoriei who may be able to help you. I shall arrange a consultation with him.'

'Thank you, Eduard. It will be a waste of his time and mine.'

'Why is that?'

'Because I cannot be cured of whatever disease you think afflicts me – if afflict me it does.'

'I made no mention of disease.'

'Is he a Freudian analyst? Is he, by any chance, a Jew?'

I guessed, to judge by my cousin's embarrassment, that he was.

'I have no need of his help or assistance or guidance. I am happy as I am.'

For the first time in many years, my father pleaded with me to honour and respect Elena Grigorescu's memory.

'She would be shocked – no, more than shocked, horrified – to hear you say that you are happy to declare that you are a – I have no wish to pronounce the word—'

'Pervert,' Cousin Eduard suggested.

'That will suffice.'

'I am happy to be Dinu Grigorescu,' I said. 'The son of Cezar and Elena. That is the extent of my current happiness.'

I tried to look serene. I was determined not to be frightened or upset by their accusations. I had progressed beyond Orthodox guilt towards a state of mind that was attuned to my love – which from the start had intimated that it would transcend lust – for the Răzvan I had left weeping at the station.

'You are enamoured of this peasant, I fear.'

Oh, that choice of word: *peasant*. It implied subjugation, ignorance, centuries of servility.

'The peasant to whom you are referring so unkindly is a cultivated man, as my cousin will testify.'

'I can testify that he speaks with obvious refinement, Cezar. I can certainly say that in his defence.'

'Defence? What defence?'

'He has the manners of the salon, to be sure. He could pass for a gentleman were it not for his features.'

It was as if Albert Le Cuziat, the snob beyond *pareil*, was speaking.

'His face proclaims his ancestry, which is that of the woods and fields. He looks like a son of the soil despite his patent sophistication.'

Listening to Cousin Eduard's patent nonsense, I began to understand why Răzvan, in the role of Honoré, insulted and humiliated his aristocratic clients. It was their turn to experience abasement, even if they were paying for it. By denying them his peasant's body, the strong-boned and muscled body of his ancestors, he was exacting a sweet revenge on their complacent forefathers, who had been content to function in a restricted feudal system which guaranteed into eternity that the poor remained poor while the already and always rich flourished. They anticipated that my lover would be rough with them, but he plied them instead with polished insults. How they must have squirmed as he demonstrated, for their startled edification, not roughness, not brutishness, but a culture superior to their own. He knew, by heart, poems they had never read; could talk of paintings and church interiors they had only been afforded a cursory glance of, and of music by composers to whom he had been introduced – Saint-Saëns, for example, and the young Maurice Ravel. And all the while he was unattainable. The son of the soil refused to be contaminated and defiled by the pomaded and scented men who had heard that Honoré provided a unique service. It occurred to me as I reflected on Răzvan's assumption of Honoré that my father and my cousin had heard tell of his anarchic activities. I allowed myself a smile at the notion.

I was aware that I was making history, private history, when I declared, in the drawing-room of the house near Cişmigiu, that I was deeply and irretrievably in love with Răzvan Popescu. I could not imagine life with anyone else. If there were to be tragic consequences, I would face them. I would die for him, I said, aware even as I did so that I was being melodramatic. The confession was a large factor in the enjoyment I felt at being honest.

'We will talk in the morning,' said my father. 'We must devise a plan to preserve, or restore, your reputation.'

My father's plan for my restoration was not immediately forthcoming. He had been embarrassed by my passionate declaration. There was still the likelihood, he insisted on reminding me, that I might marry. Elisabeta was entranced by me before she met George Văduva, but there were plenty of girls who considered Dinu Grigorescu a 'catch'. A sham marriage was a marriage just the same. The world need not know it was a deception.

'But I should know it was. I cannot picture myself as a contented deceiver.'

'What has contentment to do with it, Dinu? You could provide me with a grandson and then conduct your affairs discreetly without your wife knowing anything about them.'

'Are you speaking from experience, Tată?'

'Your mother was more devoted to her son and her God than she was to her husband. That is all I intend to say on the subject. Men have done worse things than enter into a marriage of convenience. I shall be blunt with you. It would be convenient for my reputation, and for yours, if you married an attractive woman.'

'Why attractive?'

'Because you are an attractive man, in appearance at least, and society here in Bucharest would find it perplexing if you attached yourself to a frump, however amiable her disposition.'

'I promise that I shall never wed a frump. I can give you that assurance with heartfelt confidence.'

After a time, my father informed his colleagues and acquaintances that I had decided to remain a 'confirmed bachelor', a combination of words that signified I was a callous soul whose appreciation of women never progressed in the direction of the altar. I would continue to be a constant temptation to the fairer sex. I was not alone in my predilection.

I went on wearing the clothes Amalia chose and bought for me. I dressed plainly, though, whenever I had myself photographed for Răzvan. I cared to look decadent in the company of men and women in Bucharest to whom I was either moderately affectionate or completely indifferent, but I knew beyond doubt that the beauty Răzvan detected in me, and treasured, required no adornment or decoration. I was his in anything casual there was to hand.

Răzvan abandoned the art of the cryptic postcard message and wrote me letters, varying in length and substance, instead. They came in monthly instalments. They were mostly professions of his undying love for Dinicu, but occasionally he told me of chance encounters with famous artists who were aware, after many years, of Prince E's educative involvement with him. One such was the shy and strange Constantin Brâncuşi, who had been struck by the very features my cousin Eduard deplored or lamented – I wasn't sure which. The retiring and modest sculptor had drawn his fellow peasant's face from several angles, with the intention of sculpting an imposing figure of him, perhaps. He captured his eyes, his nose, his chin and his always unruly hair in the drawing I am looking at as I write. It is a work of spontaneous genius.

My lover assured me of his faithfulness and I believed him. Our right hands were either happily or regretfully employed: his in rue de Dunkerque, mine in the ostentatiously elegant Carmen Sylva 4. We were united, in our special way, before the anticipated reunion that would see us entwined for ever, as we envisaged hopefully.

What had I to report to Răzvan? I began with my Cousin Eduard's return to Bucharest and his new-found contempt for Jewish bankers, politicians and businessmen. I recorded my dismay on hearing him express these thoughtless, hitherto uncharacteristic opinions, with which my father appeared to concur. In that first letter to my beloved after our tearful separation, I commented also on Cezar Grigorescu's proud description of his son as a 'confirmed bachelor' intent on breaking women's hearts. I did not say, yet, that I had made a confession to Cezar and Eduard of my love for Răzvan Popescu.

I retrieved the photograph of the prince's boy from its hiding place and put it on my bedside table. There was no cause for secrecy now.

'You should be grateful to your wicked stepmother, Dinu.'

'Why is that, Amalia?'

'Where must I begin? When you were foolish enough or courageous enough – let's say foolishly courageous – to tell the truth to Cezar and that oily man Eduard Vasiliu about your friendship with the notorious Popescu, your father was incensed. He was spitting his rage at me for an eternity-and-a-half before I contrived to calm him down.'

We were taking breakfast together, relishing the delicately bitter taste of Dundee marmalade which she had purchased at Dragomir, the city's most fashionable grocery store. I was always reminded of Dragomir when I shopped, not too often, at Fauchon in Paris. In both culinary palaces you could buy smoked fish and caviar and teas from India and the Orient and game preserved in its own aspic. Dragomir disappeared when Romania displayed its talent for farcical brutality for a shameful decade or more, but Fauchon survives, in a liberated Paris.

'It was your caring Amalia, my sweet, who chanced upon the "confirmed bachelor" cliché when Cezar's anger was at its immoderate height. "Spread the news abroad," I said to him, "that your beautiful son is intent on being a Don Juan, a philanderer – for the time being, anyway. Tell everyone that your precious only son is cast in the Byronic mould." My darling boy, by rescuing you from Cezar's wrath, I fear I have created greater havoc for you. You will be hunted and hounded by a thousand frustrated Dianas whose husbands bore them to near-extinction in the bedroom. Be warned, Dinu, of the sexual dangers ahead.'

Was it possible for me to love Elena, my devout mother, as well as this woman who was in every way her opposite? I was beginning to think it was. Even if I had hated Amalia, which I was tempted to when I was introduced to her with the terrible news that I was to be her stepson, I could still enjoy her worldly company. Unlike Elena, she did not expect goodness to be prevalent in human affairs. Amalia used the word 'wicked' almost as a term of endearment.

Whenever she called me a 'wicked boy' I knew she was complimenting me on what she described as a 'delicious misdemeanour'. My holiday in Eforie, the reason for which was at first a secret from my father, was a misdemeanour she found especially appetizing.

'Break all the laws and commandments you can,' she had advised me on the night before I set off for Constanţa. 'May you and the prince's boy have the naughtiest of naughty holidays.'

Eduard's remarks at the dining table that summer evening in 1932 offered a relatively mild foretaste of the talk that could be heard in restaurants and bars and in certain departments at the university for the remainder of the decade and beyond. It began in a muted, even embarrassed, fashion, with whispers and innuendo, before it prospered into open, unapologetic virulence. Its subject was the Jew and the nature of his Jewishness, which meant the amassing of vast sums of money and the destruction of the Christian faith.

On the first of February 1934 I attended the belated Romanian premiere of Wagner's *Tristan und Isolde*. We sat in splendour in one of the larger boxes at the opera house – my father and stepmother, Elisabeta and the poet George Văduva, with whom she was demonstrably infatuated, and Eduard Vasiliu and his new wife, Anca. The performance commenced at eight, I recall, and as I listened to the Prelude I realized that this was a work I might be enamoured of for ever. It was sung in Romanian, so there were occasions when the words and the music sounded almost estranged from each other. Tristan was sung by the divinely named Nicu Apostolescu and Isolde by Mimi Nestorescu, who shrieked on the highest notes. I was transported, even so.

We drank champagne throughout the evening, served by the sommelier from the restaurant Capşa. In the first interval, my father commented on the stupidity of the plot, while Amalia complained about the drabness of the costumes.

'There really are no clothes to speak of in Wagner. Those shifts may conceal an excess of flesh but they are not, definitely not, a pleasure to look at for hours on end. And why should the men be dressed in grey?'

'I cannot answer that question, Amalia. Perhaps it is a tradition.'

'We never have this problem with Mozart and Puccini. They are both so colourful. And so is the enchanting Franz Lehár,' she added, winking at me. 'I have a soft spot for Lehár.'

I knew why. For three happy months in 1931, Amalia had been the mistress of Rudolf Peterson, who was born Rudi Petrescu, the great tenor who specialized in operetta. She would have left Cezar for him, but he was the confirmed bachelor I was merely pretending to be.

In the second interval, when Eduard and Anca had woken up, Amalia – studying the distinguished audience with the aid of her lorgnette – remarked suddenly that there were two strange men at the back of the dress circle.

'They are not wearing black ties like everyone else. They have come in green shirts. Why were they allowed to enter the auditorium?'

Perhaps that was the first appearance in public of the green-shirted men who would blight our nation. In retrospect, their choice of music was prescient, since it was revealed some years later that *Tristan und Isolde* held a high place in Adolf Hitler's musical pantheon.

It was while I was listening to Nestorescu struggling

with the *Liebestod* that the thought came to me that Răzvan and I, without the encouragement of a love potion, were in some way doomed. I shrugged it off as a romantic fantasy, this idea of our being united in fervent sex and even more fervent dying. Such extremes of feeling were unnatural, I reasoned, and morbid. It was as absurd as it was repellent, yet it stayed with me, like a mental leech, for days.

Those green shirts, so incongruous in that dinner-jacketed, black-tied throng, were to become familiar in our unhappy country a year later. They signalled membership of the Iron Guard, a political party led by a fanatic named Codreanu, who had been inspired by St Michael, no less, to protect and preserve the purity of the Romanian people. Purity? What purity? The Romans conquered and occupied Dacia, and then the Greeks, the Turks, the Slavs, the Hungarians and the Germans occupied our land, planting their semen wherever they desired. Such was, and is, our purity.

One evening, in April, I came home from the university to be greeted in the hallway by Denisa, who informed me that a French gentleman by the name of Honoré had telephoned.

'Did he leave a message?'

'Only that he would try calling you again.'

I lifted the receiver three times and heard the voices of the family doctor, saying that he would visit Doamna Grigorescu on Friday at noon when his surgery was closed; the poet Văduva, who wished to speak to Elisabeta; and the apprentice lawyer who had witnessed my reluctant parting from Răzvan. He had news for my father, in the form of fresh evidence, concerning the case they were involved in at present. I passed the cringing Judas on to his master.

The fourth, and last, call came at around midnight, when I began to wonder if Honoré had abandoned the idea of phoning me.

It was he. It was Honoré. He was coming to Bucharest. He had booked a room in a modest hotel on a quiet street where we would be safe from prying gossips. The pretend father was more desperate than ever to embrace his pretend son. We would be together very, very soon.

The Hotel Minerva was unprepossessing. You could walk past it, thinking it was just another house on a street where all the houses looked identical. The room Răzvan had been allotted was so small as to be minute. The walls were thin. We conducted our loving navigations with a Trappist monk's disdain for noise. Our every sigh had to be measured. We didn't cry out in ecstasy. We didn't even speak.

We ate, drank and talked in a nearby taverna. A trust fund Prince E had set up for him when he was still taking lessons from Alin Dănescu had recently matured and he was now a little bit richer.

'Come and live with me, Dinicu, before I have to walk with the aid of a stick.'

'That day is in the distant future.'

'Is it? I shall be fifty in 1939. The years are running away from us. I want to spend at least some of them with you. Come back with me, dearest.'

'I wish I could,' I said, feebly. 'I will come to you, Răzvănel, I promise, as soon as I can.'

'And when, precisely, is that?'

'It is impossible to be precise. In a few months. Yes, in a few months. I have commitments at the university to honour. I will come to you. I will make sure that our bed linen smells again of lavender.'

He did not believe me and, at that exact moment, I did not believe myself either. I think I detected hatred in his eyes.

'I have enough money for both of us to live well.'

'I have to work, Răzvănel. It is a compulsion. My dream of being a poet or novelist was abandoned, cast aside, when I returned to Bucharest after our wonderful summer. I am a serious scholar, with students dependent upon my hard-earned knowledge. Oh, I am sounding so pompous.'

'Yes, you are.'

'Then I apologize.'

'So you should.'

Seeing him there, so overcome with what I knew to be sorrow, I was suddenly reckless.

'I will come to Paris next year. I will clear my desk, as the Americans say. I promise you. I really and truly and most sincerely promise you.'

'You had better.'

'I should like to go back with you to your cell. I feel a strong need for silent communion.'

I left Bucharest, and Romania, for ever in October 1935. I have to thank history for reuniting me with Răzvan – the principal irony in this narrative – because the city of my birth had become insufferable to me. I felt that I was being invited to perform in a deadly farce, in which decent citizens, the very pillars of society, were transformed into apologists for bigotry and mindless venom. My father was one such citizen, as was my devious, and deviously charming, Cousin Eduard. Cezar Grigorescu, I came to understand, was an astute practitioner of the art of grovelling to those in power, regardless of their ideals and beliefs. Their squalid views were his, too. It suddenly seemed as if the resolutely frivolous Amalia was one of the few sane people in Bucharest society.

I had been contributing articles and reviews to the moderately liberal magazine *Cuvântul* for three years. I was a respected name in literary circles because of the long essays I had written on Proust (which contained a glancing reference to Albert Le Cuziat) and Balzac and Dostoevsky (in French translation) and many Romanian writers, including the young George Văduva, whose imagist poetry, uncontaminated by politics, excited and moved me.

But now, in the autumn of 1935, *Cuvântul* had forsaken whatever liberal convictions it had once possessed. Its most distinguished reviewer, the essayist, playwright and novelist Mihail Sebastian, whose real name was Iosif Hechter, suffered the humiliation of having his pieces rejected or censored to the point of travesty. He had been made aware that he was Jewish, when hitherto he had regarded himself – if he had ever regarded himself – as a member of the human race. The editor of *Cuvântul* no longer wanted his thoughts on books by Jewish writers, paintings by Jewish artists, music by Jewish composers.

I had made friends with a brilliant professor at the university, whose passion for Shakespeare and the English poets of the sixteenth century is expressed in two books now regarded as classics: *The Man Who Was Iago* and *Brightness Falling from the Air*. He was a gentle, modest soul, unconcerned with his physical appearance, whose love for the masterpieces of the Elizabethan age was manifested in his unexpectedly sonorous voice, which struck everyone who heard it as too deep and powerful for his skinny frame. He was the first academic to be insulted by the men sporting green shirts, who had painted, in red ink, the two words Dirty Jew on the door of his office. Ion refused to be disheartened. He had, at the age of fifty-eight, a 'ripeness is all' philosophy. He knew from diligent study of the dramatist he revered above all others, that men and women are unfathomable victims and slaves to circumstance. Today's hero is tomorrow's tyrant. He was, he reasoned, a dirty Jew to those who were drawn to the idea of dirtiness being an essential element of Jewishness, and if that was their opinion, considered or not, then so be it.

I owe my survival, such as it is, to Ion Rohrlich. It was he who suggested that we leave what he called the 'devil's own country'. He had connections, thanks to his incomparable scholarship, abroad. I travelled with him, by aeroplane, to Paris, where he had secured a lectureship at the Sorbonne. He was neither surprised nor disturbed by Răzvan greeting me with an excess of affection at Orly airport.

I introduced my lover to Professor Rohrlich.

'You must take good care of my dear friend Dinu.'

'I shall. Taking good care of him will be my vocation.'

We parted at Gare du Nord, where Ion was met by his son Avram, a well-built young man whose fascination with sport and sport alone his father found incomprehensible.

'His handshake is much stronger than Marcel Proust's,' Răzvan observed when we had parted from them.

We dined at Café Larivière that evening, that same restaurant where I had been entertained so often by Eduard Vasiliu. It was there he had taken me for luncheon on the day I disgraced Cezar Grigorescu with my unmanly behaviour at Mme Laurette's world-famous establishment. I would have no cause to be spurning Sonia's advances after dinner, I thought, and smiled.

'Why are you smiling, Dinicu?'

'I was remembering that I lunched here with Eduard before he escorted me to Mme Laurette's. I hope to get home safely tonight.'

'I found your cousin rude and arrogant. I have rarely felt the urge to hit someone as much as I did when he interrupted us on rue des Trois-Frères that day.'

'He is worse than rude and arrogant now. He has become a beast.'

I had called his apartment home, for that is what it was for me. We were contained within its walls. It was no longer a temporary paradise. We could live here contentedly at last.

We had been in each other's arms on the familiar bed for uncounted moments when he remarked that I had neglected to thank him for the surprise present he had given me.

'What surprise? What present? What are you talking about?'

'Sniff.'

I did so.

'What is that smell, Dinicu?'

'It's lavender.'

'Of course it is. It is the smell that greeted me when I woke up in your garret for the first time eight years ago.'

'Thank you.'

'I asked the laundress to sprinkle lavender water on the sheets. Has she done her work to your satisfaction?'

She had.

Răzvan had tried, and failed, to write the opening chapter of his memoir. The very thought of Prince E's short life, which came to its tragic end in an obscure English hotel, still upset him deeply. The words that came reluctantly to his tongue vanished into nowhere whenever he lifted his pen. The story was too personal, too private, to be accounted for in a book to be read by strangers. Whatever he wrote would be inadequate. It was a ridiculous idea that had come to him after he had drunk far too much wine in Eforie. It was a folly, a nonsense.

Although he had enough money to live on, he continued to work at *Les Deux Cygnes*. I would meet him there most evenings, after a day spent writing reviews for two prestigious French newspapers. My mentor Ion Rohrlich had recommended me to the literary editors and they seemed to be pleased with what I wrote for them. The French have always lauded Romanian writers, so I became an expert on Petrescu and Istrati and whoever was being translated.

My father and I had disowned one another, which meant that the only domestic news – the gossip, in truth – I received from Carmen Sylva 4 came in the long and rambling letters Amalia sent to the wicked boy who was enamoured of an even more wicked man. The light-hearted, the frivolous indeed, often see and hear more than the serious people among us, who take their seriousness seriously. Amalia could not help being observant. Her eyes and ears were attuned to all the cadences and the very few nuances of blind hatred. She was appalled and amused. She contrived, in her correspondence, to make the unfunny funny.

I had left the clothes she had chosen and bought for me behind in Bucharest. Now that I lived with Răzvan, I had no reason to flaunt myself. Besides, I was no longer a member of a high society of the kind Amalia cared to move in. I was content to be a self-effacing scholar, devoting my intellectual energy to the writings of men and women I revered. I knew my literary place and it was only loosely a creative one.

I began to take English lessons, on Ion's advice, from an elderly couple, husband and wife, who had spent most of their working lives in London as correspondents for Reuters, the international news syndicate. Olivier and Catherine chain-smoked, frequently sharing the same foul-smelling cigarettes, as they explicated what on first uneasy acquaintance seemed inexplicable. I could not understand why the combination of the letters o,u,g and h should represent myriad different sounds. They had faced the same problem when they were young, they assured me.

Mine was, I told myself, even in those moments of utter darkness when it is said one experiences a dark night of the soul, a charmed life. I was sharing an apartment with my beloved. I was already an esteemed critic, and yet I could not shake off the bouts of despair that were visited upon me. Were they my mother's legacy to me? Was her son betraying her with Răzvan? These were silly, improbable questions, I reasoned, yet I found myself attempting to answer them many more times than I wished. I mentioned none of these misgivings to my prince's boy, the prince's unmistakeably middle-aged man, as we lay together in our lavender-scented happiness.

We were as good as married. We welcomed each other's homecomings with kisses and hugs. Although I was still young, a mere 27, I felt that I had settled into an enduring liaison. We would stay inseparable, with only death dividing us. So I decided when we celebrated Christmas in 1935.

It is easier to describe the bewitchment I felt on meeting Honoré in Albert Le Cuziat's Palace of Iniquity than it is to set down the day-to-day dealings of our coexistence on rue de

Dunkerque. Our passion was muted now, was accepted as a fact, a pleasurable and ordinary fact, rather than the dangerous and exciting adventure we had embarked upon in the summer of 1927. There were entire nights when exploration was almost too tiresome to contemplate. Our bodies belonged to the two of us. We had become mutual, and still loving, friends. We slept, often enough, contentedly.

One day in April, after a two-hour class with Olivier and Catherine, I decided to eat in a small, but much admired, restaurant. I had been seated at a corner table for only a matter of minutes when I looked up from the menu and saw Albert Le Cuziat smiling down on me.

'This is a delightful surprise, Domnule Grigorescu.'

'It is a surprise for me, too. I thought you only took luncheon at the Ritz.'

'Not today. I am not in aristocratic company. I wouldn't be seen dead at the Ritz in the company of my fellow diner. I believe you are acquainted with Mme Laurette?'

'I had a brief conversation with her once.'

'She is very, very wealthy. I am sure I can persuade her to pay for your meal if you join us – Silviu, is it?'

'Dinu.'

'Would you care to join us, Dinu?'

'Yes. But you do not have to inveigle Mme Laurette into paying for me.'

I followed the Pandarus who had altered my life so dramatically to another, larger table. I bowed to Mme Laurette, who raised her champagne glass to me. Her hair was more fiercely orange than I remembered it. Perhaps she had dyed it afresh for M. Albert's delectation.

'Give the boy some Clicquot, Albert,' she commanded.

'Of course, of course.'

The two brothel keepers wished me good health. I wished them the same.

'We are too old and too immoral to be healthy,' said Mme Laurette.

'That is true, my dear. That is far too true for comfort.'

The pair of them cackled at this remark. I saw that Albert's teeth had turned a darker shade of yellow.

'You are residing in Paris at the moment?'

'I am, Mme Laurette.'

'Do you wish that I should address you as Alexandru?'

'My name is Dinu. I was Alexandru for one afternoon only. You have an extraordinary memory.'

'Not at all. It is my business to remember every success and every failure. You were one of the latter, bless you. You failed dismally.'

'I know I did.'

'And how is the insatiable M. Gérard?'

'I am sorry, but I am unacquainted with the gentleman you mention.'

'He was your chaperon, so to speak, on the day of the disaster.'

I had forgotten that M. Gérard was the assumed name of my cousin Eduard.

'Eduard Vasiliu is employed by the National Bank in Romania. I believe he has abandoned Paris and London for good.'

'I always charged him extra for his tastes. My poor petite Louise had to recuperate for two or three days after he had had his fun with her.'

'He is married now.'

'I pity his wife.'

'Do not waste your pity, Madame. She is as obnoxious as her husband.'

'You sound as if you hate him.'

'I despise him. I think "despise" is more apropos than "hate". He speaks of nothing but the supposed infamy of the Jews.'

'That is unwise of him,' said M. Albert. 'I would have closed down my Pagoda of Pleasure aeons ago were it not for my Jewish customers.'

'I do so agree, Albert. Naming no names—'

'As is our way, Laurette—'

'Naming no names, but we are grateful to our circumcised clients for their generosity and exquisite manners. They treat my girls with respect. There was one – do you recall, Albert? – who visited both our establishments on the same day. What shall we call him? "M. Ruben" will serve, I think. Yes, he favoured variety, did he not?'

'He most certainly did. He was one of my Safarovians, if you understand me.'

They cackled again. They would have been peerless as the witches in *Macbeth*, I thought.

I was alternately entranced and bemused by them. I cannot remember, as I write, what exactly we ate and drank. It was beef, probably, with a fine claret.

'Is Safarov's replacement proving satisfactory?'

'Oh, you naughty Romanian beauty. My Louis with the sunken chest is proving himself to be an equal to the Russian bear in almost every department of cruelty. The industrialist has had a stroke but not, thanks be to God, on my premises. He has been superseded by a Jewish gentleman – shall we call him M. Jacobs? – who is positively awestruck by what the brute does to him. I hope and pray that romance is not in the offing, as it was with you and Honoré.'

'Honoré, Albert? Are you referring to the prince's boy?'

'I am indeed, Laurette.'

'And is he this palely beautiful creature's lover?

'He is, my dear.'

'Then it is no wonder that he resisted Sonia. Is the prince's boy as roguishly handsome as he was when I last saw him?'

I said 'He is' and M. Albert said 'He is not.'

'You still resemble Rudolph Valentino, Dinu.'

'If that is a compliment, Mme Laurette, I accept it.'

'Oh, how coy you are. You look in the mirror when you are shaving, do you not?'

'Every morning.'

'Then you must see what I see and what I see pleases me.'

'It pleases me too, Laurette. I have offered him employment, but he has resisted and rejected my kindness, the silly, love-stricken youth.'

This observation provided the cue for more cackling. I wondered if I had strayed into a painting by Hieronymus Bosch, with these ancient demons on either side of me.

'I am a serious man, M. Albert. I am a scholar.'

'I am more than aware that you are. I read your article on my dearest Marcel. It is thanks to him that I am in business.'

'I know.'

'And you are not disapproving?'

It was then that I surprised myself.

'I am not disapproving, M. Albert. How could I be?'

Although I heard Elena chastising me, I continued: 'Your dearest Marcel, my endlessly diverting Proust, is beyond accepted morality. He understands the complexities of human nature. That knowledge is his special gift. My father considers me a pervert, as does my cousin Eduard, alias M. Gérard. They are blinkered. I am who I am, and I have Proust to thank for that self-discovery.'

'There speaks the essayist, would you not agree, Laurette?'

'He has an elegant turn of phrase.'

'He is a divine fool otherwise. His devotion to the prince's boy, whilst laudable, makes me fear for his judgment.'

'You are such a dreadful cynic, Albert. Were you never in love?'

'I endured an infatuation during my reckless late adolescence. Once I had recovered from it, I gave my heart a severe telling-off. It learnt the lesson immediately. No further education was required.'

'Oh, Dinu, just listen to the old deceiver. He and I have lived so long in our profitable world of make-believe that we tend to forget what kind of love-scarred wrecks we were before we ventured into business. Those early heartbreaks inspired us to replace unrequited affection with the comfort money brings.'

'Did I hear you say the dread word "profitable", Laurette? If it had not been for the industrialist and his Wednesday persecutions, I would have had to close down the *Bains* a decade ago. I am tempted to weep at the thought of the thousands upon thousands of francs I have counted out to the police when they have threatened to arrest me. You have not suffered that particular ignominy, I believe.'

'I am pleased to tell you that I have not. Many of my regular visitors are upholders of the law. The considerate hostess who is Mme Laurette favours them with a special discount in recognition of their service to the community.'

'Ah, the saintly Laurette. You charge the policemen less

and keep your profits rising by asking the bankers and politicians to pay more.'

'You are being fanciful, Albert.'

'And you would have been burnt at the stake in the Middle Ages, alongside the Maid of Orléans.'

Their cackling was louder and more raucous. They looked at each other benevolently as they laughed.

Encouraged by the excessive amount of wine I had drunk, I invited Mme Laurette to describe the nature of M. Gérard's, or Cousin Eduard's, peculiar tastes, which caused Louise to need two or three days of recuperation.

She slapped the back of my hand. 'Impertinent child, I have been indiscreet enough for one day. You cannot expect me to answer such a bold question. Your cousin's tastes are not peculiar at all. I speak to you as an expert. M. Gérard is simply a little too energetic. In the interests of discretion, I cannot – and shall not – reveal more.'

'I apologize, Madame, for my brashness.'

'That is graceful of you.'

It transpired that Mme Laurette always drank Veuve Clicquot at the beginning and end of her 'excursions', as she deemed her rare visits to expensive restaurants. We returned to champagne for our desserts. Albert Le Cuziat looked sober, but his friend confessed that she was seeing both of us double. There were two jaded Alberts and a pair of blissful young men.

'Since our Havens of Happiness are closed today, we have every excuse to enjoy some freedom from duty.'

'We are of one mind, Albert, even though I am looking at two of you. I am sure we will be playing to full houses, to use a theatrical expression, tomorrow.'

'Shall I propose a toast, Laurette?'

'Please do.'

'To frustrated men.'

'Let us clink and drink to that.'

So the three of us raised and clinked our glasses to the frustrated men who visited the two houses of costly sin. I had been of their number once, I reminded myself.

Mme Laurette paid the bill, as Albert had anticipated.

'My friend is the meanest, most miserly, person in the entire world, Dinu. I think I should die if I ever saw him bring out his wallet and leave a few francs on the table. He loved his mother and she loved him and that is the best thing anyone could say regarding Albert Le Cuziat.'

'You hurt me, Laurette. You wound me.'

'Hurt you? Wound you, you old beast? You are beyond hurting and wounding.'

They were in agreement again, and they cackled accordingly.

Mme Laurette insisted that we share a French kiss before she stumbled into her cab. I duly obliged.

Albert Le Cuziat said farewell. If I ever wanted to reconsider his offer of employment, I knew where to come.

'Thank you, M. Albert.'

'My felicitations and curses to Honoré.'

These were the last words I heard them speak. He died two years later. Then Mme Laurette was strangled by a burglar she had surprised early in the morning attempting to open her safe.

In Eforie, on our enchanted holiday, Răzvan had surprised me with his craven fear of thunder and lightning. Whenever a storm was about to happen, usually after six or seven bakingly hot days, I would treat him as if he were my child, cuddling him in the darkest corner of our apartment, until the rumbling noises and terrifying flickers of light abated. He shivered and sometimes wept in my arms.

I discovered, now that I was living by his side for weeks and months that would soon grow into years, that Răzvan was afraid of other things as well. A spider making its dainty, silent way out of a plughole in the kitchen sink caused him to tremble in a manner I found laughable.

'Kill it,' he shouted.

'It isn't a tarantula, Răzvan. It won't harm you.'

'It scares me.'

I coaxed the insect on to a sheet of white paper and deposited it on the windowsill, leaving it to fend for itself. I shut the window, to ensure that it wouldn't return to alarm my beloved.

'Calm yourself.'

I could cope with thunderstorms and spiders, but I was to find myself angry with him on those occasions, increasing in number, when he expressed his wish to die. He would quote Eminescu's phrase *dor de moarte*, 'longing for death', as if it were his one remaining hope.

'You are insulting and degrading me when you are feeling mawkish. You are aware, are you not, that we are united in love and that if you achieve your ambition and attain your precious gift then I shall be desolated? You are aware, perhaps?'

'You will be a happier man without me.'

Ah, here was marriage at last. The overture had sounded on the marital strife we had been confident would never be ours. We were not mismatched, like the couples in so many of the novels and stories we treasured. We were not promiscuous. We had employed our right hands throughout our long separations. We were intended for each other from the moment we met in Albert Le Cuziat's Den of Disrepute.

'I will not be a happier man without you. You know as much, if you know anything. Please, please stop.'

I wanted the overture to end abruptly, in mid-flow, and to my gratification it did.

'I am sorry, my sweet. There are times, God help me, when I think only of myself, and this was one of them.'

There were to be many more such times. I became a wearily unhappy Cassandra, predicting when the next morose outpouring would come. Accomplished sage that I was, I often stopped him seconds in advance of the words I anticipated.

'Răzvan, I beg you, do not give me your longing-for-death aria again. I am sick of it, my dearest. It bores me.'

However melancholic he was, however dissatisfied I was with his perpetual gloom, we still used those terms of endearment which had once come so naturally and speedily to our lips. They were lifeboats for us in 1936, when Răzvan's despair first asserted itself as a constant in our household. I was still his Dinicu or Dinuleţ, he my Răzvănel.

But thunderstorms and spiders were minuscule concerns, as nothing almost, when compared with his dread of illness and the necessity of consulting a doctor and – terror of all terrors – being confined in a hospital ward amongst the sick and dying. He, who had held and stroked and kissed his mother's hand on her deathbed, as he related to me, could not countenance even the idea of Răzvan Popescu succumbing to anything more than a mild headache or a stomach in temporary upheaval.

'You look very tired, Răzvănel.'

'Let me prove to you that I am not,' he responded, pulling me into bed.

We are, I thought, like old lovers now, stopping and starting, while he recaptured his breath, where once – nearly ten years ago – we had been gymnastic for magical nights on end. Perseverance had replaced exploration and navigation. He persevered while I held him to me, loving him as one who knows that he is going to lose – not too soon; in the very distant future, perhaps – the very object of all his earthly desires. I wiped the copious sweat from his face and chest and curled into him, as happy as I could be with a deeply unhappy man. It seemed enough to satisfy the two of us, for the moment.

Amalia continued to write about everyday life in Bucharest with as much good humour as she could command. It lessened with each letter. I sensed there were shadows behind her comic observations. In fact, I knew there were, though she tried to hide or ignore them. The newspapers I wrote for kept me informed of the sinister events that were happening daily in the city of my birth. It had become the fashion to despise and denigrate Jews and my father was nothing if not fashionable. Amalia had loathed Eduard on first meeting and she rarely mentioned him, except to observe sarcastically that he had transferred his allegiance from the purity of Romanian blood to the sanctity of the Romanian soul. That, she conceded, was some kind of progress.

I garnished the truth in my replies. It was as if Răzvan and I were Orlando and Rosalind in a Parisian Forest of Arden. I was my usual bookish self, no longer the dandy she had tried to cultivate, and my lover was happy in his job at *Les Deux Cygnes*. A certain primness in my nature prevented me describing the meal I had relished in the bizarre company of Mme Laurette and M. Albert, even as I was aware that it would amuse her. I was a liberated spirit, but there were limitations.

We celebrated the year's end with Ion and Avram in Brasserie Lipp. Răzvan, who was sober and apprehensive at the start of the dinner, soon became confident enough to speak seriously in Ion's beguiling presence. I learned much that evening about Răzvan's past. He told Ion, in detail, of his two meetings with Proust – how the master had invited him to describe peasant life on the estate at Corcova, and that the novelist had listened to him with unfeigned interest, and that Proust had congratulated him on his, Răzvan's, knowledge of Gothic architecture. 'You are, truly, the prince's protégé,' he had said, with the slightest of smiles.

Răzvan had befriended, briefly, the son of the composer Georges Bizet, but had decided that Jacques's dangerous behaviour was too unsettling to live with. 'He had a gun, which he either pointed at my head or at his own. Whose would it be? Was he contemplating suicide or murder, or both? In his rare moments of normality, he was charming and sophisticated, but the streak of madness in him eventually frightened me away.'

Here, beyond the confining space of our apartment, was my intelligent, optimistic, even carefree lover, the Răzvan from whom I had been estranged for months. Here he was, talking to someone he scarcely knew, with the excitement and enthusiasm that had been missing from his voice for all the time of our domestic estrangement. He sounded and looked revivified. I was momentarily jealous of Ion's capacity to bring him back from the realms of the living dead. I envied the gift my friend possessed for finding warmth of feeling where there had been coldness and indifference. I no longer had that gift, it seemed, outside the bedroom walls.

Avram, apart from expressing the traditional courtesies, said nothing all evening.

The date is for ever with me. On the sixteenth of February 1937, Răzvan woke up beside me, weeping. I asked him what was wrong.

He had dreamt of his mother, seeing her before he was born, dancing to gypsy music with the man who might have been his father. They were sprightly, they were happy. It was a summer's night. Behind them was the little church, where the two princes and their mother worshipped alongside their peasants. Was it Angela's marriage to Ilie that was being celebrated? It certainly looked like a wedding feast. Then Prince E appeared, with his face undamaged, younger even than Răzvan had known him. Angela kissed his outstretched, gloved hand, and the man who might have been Răzvan's father bowed deeply to his master. It was how things used to be.

'It sounds like a lovely dream. Why are you still weeping?'

'The only father I have had was the prince, who killed himself out of vanity and boredom. That is my paternal inheritance.'

Just weeks earlier, chatting with Ion Rohrlich, he had cast his demons aside. Now they were back again.

'If my mother had not smacked me that day and if the prince had not stopped his carriage—'

'You would not be the clever man you are.'

'I have no wish to be clever any longer. I am worn out with being educated.'

'This is nonsense, Răzvănel.'

'You will never understand.'

'I think you may be right,' I answered. 'I think you may very well be right.'

He did not go to *Les Deux Cygnes* that morning. He preferred to stay at home with his Dinicu, the man he had accused of not understanding him. I was perplexed, although I refrained from saying so.

I was at the typewriter for hours, working on a lengthy essay about contemporary Romanian poets, including George Văduva, to whom I was now strangely related. He had married Elisabeta, my stepmother's daughter, yet his poems continued to be melancholic, even mournful. They were spare and allusive and completely unfashionable in a culture that was demanding absolutes of its artists.

Then Răzvan surprised me by kissing the back of my neck and whispering his apologies. There was something dark inside him, he said, that he was unable to fathom. It came of its own sinister accord. He hoped it would pass.

There was nothing left for us to navigate, apart from our cherished memories of navigation.

In September of that same year, he stopped speaking French. The Romanian he gabbled instead was barely literate, the very language of his early childhood. It was as if he were in another, alien world.

The doctor I had summoned, the doctor he would have resisted had he been capable of resisting him, said that Răzvan had suffered a stroke. It was a miracle M. Popescu was speaking at all, even if it was – to his ears – gibberish. There were, he suspected, other complications. The patient had to be removed to hospital immediately. A hospital?

That was the one building Răzvan dreaded entering – it represented hopelessness; it was a place, once entered, you never escaped from. He had remembered a phrase from a recent American film – 'The last chance saloon' – and that was what a hospital meant to him. A last chance was a last chance, and beyond that there was nothing.

I sat by his bedside for unaccountable days and nights. Whenever he spoke it was childish babble, peasant babble, unadorned with correct grammar. It was the language he had inherited before the prince had chosen to make him his surrogate son. It was the language, at the last, of infancy.

He rose in the bed, looked at me for an unseeing second, called out to Angela, fell back and died.

I sent a telegram to Mircea, Bogdan and Irina, care of the B— estate at Corcova, informing them of their brother's sudden, unexpected death.

The funeral service was held in that same, scented Orthodox church near the Bastille I had visited in 1927, racked with senseless guilt over the pleasure I had shared with Honoré, soon to be Răzvan. Ion Rohrlich, who abominated all places of worship, including synagogues, stood beside me as the open coffin was brought in. Răzvan's fellow waiters and barmen from *Les Deux Cygnes* were there, and the concierge from rue de Dunkerque, and so was my former landlady, Mlle Simone, who cried softly throughout the ceremony. I was far beyond tears myself, looking down on the man I loved, and would continue loving. I kissed his forehead and his eyelids and put my fingers to the parched lips that had once been moist. I bade him *au revoir*.

Then the coffin was closed. After the burial, the

mourners repaired to *Les Deux Cygnes* where – spurred on by Răzvan's friends – I drank myself into a stupor.

I received the reply to my telegram eight weeks later. It read DO NOT SEND BODY and was signed by D. Irimia, whoever he or she was.

Prince E's solicitor, who had been entrusted with the management of Răzvan Popescu's money and property, had persuaded my lover to write a will. The lease of the apartment would end six months after his death, but the remainder of his dowry had been left to me. It consisted of several thousand francs and the Brâncuşi drawing, a photograph of Răzvan with the prince and Marcel Proust and some letters and postcards. It was more than enough for me.

I was to be the recipient of a truly surprising gift. One morning the concierge handed me a parcel that had been delivered by a bald gentleman whom she described as having a 'disturbing smile'. I thanked her, went up to the apartment I would soon be leaving, and opened it. I took out a black box, pulled back the lid and discovered, wrapped in the softest tissue paper imaginable, a pearl necklace. Beneath it was a letter, in Albert Le Cuziat's elegant handwriting.

My dear Monsieur or Domnule Dinu Grigorescu.

The enclosed necklace came into my possession in 1897, when I was the prettiest sixteen-year-old in Paris. It was bestowed upon me by no less a personage than Prince Constantin Radziwill, who promoted me to the rank of First Footman after stealing me from another Polish prince who was neither as wealthy nor as renowned.

There were eleven subordinate footmen below me, all of whom had been presented with pearls by their appreciative and discerning master. This is not ersatz jewellery, not common paste, but the genuine, very costly, thing.

Allow me to be both brazen and flippant. You have been widowed, alas, and since it is the custom for the widow to wear black, which I presume you are doing, what better to offset the gloom than a row of gleaming pearls? The esteemed Coco Chanel herself maintains that a pearl necklace should only be worn with a simple black dress—designed by Coco, naturally. Am I offending you? I do hope not.

After Prince Constantin discarded me, I was employed as a footman by another prince, a countess, a count and a duke. I have moved and functioned in the highest circles. I did not flaunt Prince R's gift, because I knew by so doing that I would only inspire envy.

I shall be deeply offended, or as deeply offended as it is possible for Le Cuziat to be, if you reject this exceptional offering. My sobriquet for the industrialist who hero-worshipped the brutal Safarov in his curious fashion was GOD'S GIFT ON A RAINY DAY. *Look at this necklace, picture a rainy day, and remember Albert Le Cuziat gratefully in what might be the dark times to come. I have myriad aches and pains as I approach senility.*

Post Scriptum: Should you tire occasionally of your literary activities, there is a vacancy here at Les Bains for you.

Post Post Scriptum: Pectus Excavatum *is proving himself to be indispensable. M. Jacobs's appetite for everything below the sunken chest remains insatiable. Louis does not confine his activities to Wednesday afternoons, as the Russian did. He has a taste for expensive chocolates, but that is his only failing. God bless him.*

Amalia, for all her skittishness, or perhaps because of it, had understood the depth of my love for Răzvan. I had telephoned her on the evening of the funeral, an hour or so before I became completely drunk, and all she had said was

'My sweet' or 'My sweet one' or 'My dearest of stepsons'. She had blown me a telephonic kiss.

And now, in March 1938, she sent me the grimmest of grim news. Our King, Carol the Second, was enamoured of the Nazis, and Hitler was his hero. His alleged Jewish mistress, who had changed her name to Lupescu and with whom he had eloped in the 1920s, leaving his eight-year-old son Michael to occupy the throne, was living in a luxurious villa, mere yards away from the palace. Her presence there and her obvious disdain for the Romanian people had strengthened their already strong hatred of the Jews. Romania was in turmoil.

There was something worse she had to impart. George Văduva, the young poet whose work I had championed, had taken his life. The devastated Elisabeta – a widow now both in name and in fact – had discovered him hanging from a stairwell. There was no suicide note to explain – in some small measure, at least – why he had chosen to obliterate himself.

Cezar had remarked at dinner that it was the custom for poets to do such things, and Eduard – my once solicitous cousin – had laughed at this, adding that he found the man's stuff incomprehensible and out of touch with the spirit of the times.

Amalia had underlined the phrase 'the spirit of the times' with ten bold exclamation marks to accompany it.

My half-life had begun; my new and lasting half-life. I was a half-person without Răzvănel. No one else would charm me with the diminutives Dinicu and Dinuleţ ever again. I would allow no one to do so.

I had moved back into Mlle Simone's ivory tower, where

I had once tried to be a well-fed and watered bohemian. I wrote feverishly now. I accepted every commission I was offered. I sometimes assumed an expertise I did not possess, as is often the way with journalists.

Some of the books I read and reviewed were concerned with doomed or discontented lovers, but they gave me no solace, and I was glad of that. I once observed, in a gleeful mood, that the sorrowful couple deserved the deaths the author had ordained for them. They were too angelic to survive in the melodramatic world of his severely limited imagination. As I typed those disapproving words, I realized that there is nothing quite as satisfying as sarcasm to counter unhappiness.

I visited the little cemetery regularly, bearing fresh flowers, including the anemones – purple, red and white – of which he was especially fond. I talked – under my breath if there were other mourners present; out loud, if I was the only person near the white marble gravestone that bore his name and dates.

In dreams, to which I seemed more than ever prone, I had to call a truce between my beloved Răzvan and my adored mother. They fought over me, the agitated pair, declaring that I was his and I was hers, and raising their vanished voices in a perpetual squabble. Răzvan was invariably the more reasonable, talking lightly of our navigations and explorations, enraging Elena with each affectionate word. 'You are speaking to me from hell,' she admonished him, and when he riposted: 'And where are you?' she was silent. I waited for her to respond. 'Mamă, where are you?' I called to her in anguish. Her dreadful, to me dreadful, silence persisted.

*

Ion Rohrlich, my benefactor, asked me how my English was progressing. I knew it well enough, I said, to appreciate certain poems and stories.

'But will you be confident speaking it?'

'I hope to be.'

'How soon? Weeks? Months?'

'Months, I think.'

'I should like you to accompany me to London. I have been offered a lectureship there. If you can give me your guarantee that your command of the language will be just a little commanding, I propose to recommend you as my invaluable research assistant.'

I could not imagine leaving Paris, and said so.

'That is a pity. A polyglot Romanian is certain to find employment there. Besides, Avram would enjoy your company.'

'But he never says anything, particularly to me.'

'That is his way. He is fond of you.'

'Fond?'

'Precisely. If you join me in London, I will explain the nature of his fondness. It is not, I must insist, of the kind Răzvan Popescu showed you. He is a subtle creature, my son.'

I wrote to Amalia, my far-from-wicked stepmother, to tell her I was considering moving to London. Ion was to join many distinguished writers and artists who were welcomed there and he had invited me to be his research assistant.

She replied with the information that the British were loathed in Bucharest, where once – during the reign of King Ferdinand and Queen Marie – they had been adornments to society. Cezar had entertained the ambassador in our house, if I recalled. Their reluctance to espouse Hitler and his appalling cohorts did not please either of the political parties, desperate to outdo each other in their condemnation of the wandering race. She would advise me to go with Professor Rohrlich as soon as possible. London was a channel away from the continent and therefore a place of greater safety at the present.

'It is a matter of both deep sadness and optimistic happiness that Elisabeta is five months pregnant with the child the cruel George had planted in her,' she remarked in an impassioned post scriptum. His words were more precious to him than the girl he said he loved and the baby he was aware they had conceived.

We travelled by ferry to England. There were forms to fill at Dover and questions to be answered and proof was required of my academic qualifications. In 1939, and throughout the war, Romanians were a suspect species. I was twice taken blindfolded to a house outside the capital where I was interrogated for hours. Then the last of the three miracles in my life – falling in love with Răzvan; meeting and befriending Ion Rohrlich – occurred in 1941, when I was invited by the BBC World Service and Radio Free Europe to translate the broadcasts and propaganda that were coming out of Romania, France and Italy. As I sat, day after day, night after night, in the tiny studio, I hoped I was responsible for alerting the Allies to possible dangers and saving a few lives. I drank gallons of tea and ersatz, bottled coffee to keep myself awake and alert. I felt pride in acknowledging that I was responsibly employed. At my most fanciful, I thought of future generations being able to read Proust, thanks to my dedicated efforts.

Three

RĂZVAN IS AN inescapable presence, even now, some thirty years after his death. I converse with him every day. I use the word 'converse' deliberately, for I frequently hear his voice in the mornings and afternoons when I am explaining the rudiments of Romanian grammar or lecturing on my much-invaded country's bloody history to the students who have enrolled for the two courses I teach in the school of Eastern European Studies at the university. He sometimes, but not too often, corrects my mistakes. I catch him chastising me for my confident ignorance. Such is the lasting nature of our love.

What an old-fashioned, romantic creature I remain in my sixth, and final, decade. I sit in my small apartment in Marylebone, my home throughout the war against Germany, and marvel that I escaped the bomb that fell on a nearby block of flats, killing most of its occupants. I helped save a mother and child, pulling them from the rubble. I remember the woman telling me that I did not look English. Was I going to kill her? No, no, I insisted, I wasn't. I kissed her dust-covered hand, in the manner of my countrymen, and said I was proud to be in England, fighting – in my own limited way – the enemy that occupied France and had taken possession of the land of my birth. She continued to be suspicious of her rescuer until a fire fighter with a sharp London accent thanked me for being so brave and responsible. He called me his mate, and that one, almost affectionately spoken word caused her to cast aside her doubts. She expressed her gratitude, gruffly. I replied, I think, that I was only doing what a fellow human being should. Then I became embarrassed and said goodnight and walked away.

I suppose that woman, whose name I never learned, was in her rights to be wary of a foreigner. She was not alone in her wariness. I am writing this coda to my solitary book in May 1967, the year in which the doctors predict I shall die. I continue to find it absurd that, under English law, I was expected to report to a local police station at a fixed time every week to establish the fact that I was still resident in the capital and obeying the laws of the land. Because of this order, which I never ceased to honour, I formed unlikely friendships with the officers on duty, chief among whom was with the jovial Sergeant Alec Wilkins.

'How many state secrets has the Romanian spy passed on to the Soviets since our last chinwag?' he would ask as he poured strong tea into mugs and offered me two of his treasured ginger biscuits. This was our Friday afternoon ritual, with the exception of the day of Christ's fleeting descent into hell, for several years. After our meetings were officially brought to an end in 1959, I continued to see Alec as usual for the chinwag we enjoyed so much. He wondered if the Romanian spies had a word for 'chinwag'. I answered that there were two – the Turkish *tacla* and the Greek *taifas*, which means 'prattle'. Neither, I said, was as humorous as 'chinwag', with its picture of two chins wagging like the tails of cats and dogs in the excitement that the exchange of gossip provides.

Then Alec retired with his wife Elsie to a cottage he had bought in his native Yorkshire and my chinwagging days were over. Whisky replaced tea when we said our goodbyes.

'The next time you send a message to that Khrushchev bloke, tell him to watch out for Sergeant Wilkins, won't you?'

'I will, Alec, rest assured. I will scare the pants off him.'

I knew, and did not know, what was happening in my beleaguered country. My knowledge was confined to the propaganda I was paid to translate. Romania had forsaken her decadent past in the name of equality. The peasants were the new aristocrats in a society in which everyone belonged, as of natural right, to an aristocracy of human endeavour. It sounded like paradise, but I guessed it wasn't. One of the most enduring clichés came to mind: it was all 'too good to be true'.

I lived alone in a city that had just begun to restore itself to its former liveliness after years of essential austerity. There were fewer waste grounds now – those bleak reminders of where German bombs had fallen. The rationing of food and clothing was ended. The last of my ration books, with a few coupons intact, was wedged between Proust and Eminescu on the cramped shelf by my bed. It was a part of my life, as they were.

A letter I had written to Amalia in 1944 was returned to me twelve years later in an envelope indicative of state disapproval. Several harmless sentences had been underlined in red ink, for reasons only the official who had done so understood. They dealt with trivial matters – what was being performed at the Opera House, if anything; the menu at Capşa; the love-lives of friends and enemies. My expressed enthusiasm for the poems of George Văduva, who had caused her daughter such terrible anguish, inspired a riot of redness. Văduva's delicate verses, blithely unconcerned with politics and power, had offended the fascist status quo and now they were upsetting the Soviets, it seemed. To write about trees, gardens, flowers, the burgeoning of love, the threat of imminent despair, was the act of a deeply irresponsible poet, however safely dead. The logic of the malignly powerful is beyond the logic of the ordinary citizen. It functions in its own absurd universe.

My dear and trusted Ion Rohrlich died, with quiet grace, five years ago. I was at his bedside, along with Avram and his wife. He invited us to plant last kisses on him, which we did. At his secular funeral, several actors and scholars he had influenced and befriended read from *The Tempest* and *Cymbeline* and *Venus and Adonis*. What need of the mischievous and undoubting Bible, when there was Shakespeare to remind us of our transience, our joys, our hopelessness, the fragile concerns of our fragile lives? He offers us nothing more than the certainty of our own uncertainties, and that is surely enough to contemplate. This was Ion's own eulogy, delivered by the greatest Hamlet of his day, who often dined alone, as I did, at Chez Victor in Soho, with its gingham tablecloths, its hanging clusters of onion and garlic, and waiters who spoke English with Parisian accents. I could picture Răzvan beside me on the banquette, our fingers entwined as in the old days at Café Larivière.

Time is against me now, and though I doubt that many people will read this account of my life with, and without, the prince's boy, I must record some recent events that merit my attention, if no one else's. Oh, how pompous I sound. Permit me, whoever you are, to be tiresomely chronological. On the twentieth of December, 1964, to be precise, and

I am always that, I was celebrating the end of term and the beginning of the Christmas holidays in a pub in Bloomsbury. Antal, Nicolas, Corina and I had eaten fish and chips wrapped in the pages of newspapers, and there we were drinking beer underneath a photograph of a mournful Virginia Woolf. Everyone in the saloon bar that evening was on the happy verge of drunkenness.

'There is a young man staring at you, Dinu. He can't keep his eyes off you,' said the ever-observant Corina, with whom I would be celebrating the birth of Christ in five days' time, along with her English husband and their three children. 'He is very handsome, my dear. He looks serious. I am surprised you haven't noticed him.'

I returned the stranger's stare. He smiled. I wanted to return his smile, but his resemblance, his startling resemblance to Răzvan Popescu prevented me. There were the same dark eyes, the same beard, the same delicacy in the otherwise strong face. There was something close to the beauty of Răzvan within my appreciative gaze.

I turned away from that beauty, deliberately, and chatted with Antal, Nicolas and Corina about the clever and decidedly not-so-clever students we had been teaching.

'He is certainly persistent,' said Antal, who had fled from Hungary in 1956, after the Russian intervention in Budapest. 'You have made a definite conquest.'

'I am too old for conquests. I am content with my uneventful existence. I have had all I want and more of love.'

We laughed, I remember. I had persuaded them that I was a dedicated, if not desiccated, bachelor these days.

'You are still handsome,' Corina assured me. 'You are still, as the English say, a *catch*.'

'I have no intention of being caught.'

'You have bewitched him,' said Nicolas. 'He is either mad or beguiled.'

'Mad, I should say, definitely mad.'

'He is not going to tolerate you saying no for an answer, Dinu.'

'I shan't give him the opportunity to ask the question.'

I parted from my friends, kissing each of them on both cheeks, and walked none too steadily in the direction of my flat. I heard footsteps behind me and was not surprised when the man who reminded me of Răzvan was at my side.

'Hello.'

'Hello.'

'My name is William. I am Bill or Billy to people who know me well.'

'Are you?'

'You don't look English.'

'That's because I'm not.'

'What are you then?'

'A human being, I think, of the male gender.'

I stopped. I looked at him.

'What do you want, William, Bill or Billy?'

'You.'

His voice sounded nothing like Răzvan's, of course, even as he spoke with my lover's directness.

'I have abandoned physical love, William. Allow me to retire to my cubbyhole alone.'

'I refuse to allow you to escape from my clutches,' he said, smiling. He went on to say that his was a reckless nature. It was his custom, right or wrong, to throw himself in at the deep end. That's what he was doing now, because that was what he wanted. I was not to send him away unhappy.

Unhappy? I was amused by his cavalier use of the word.

Had he known unhappiness, the all-consuming demon that blights everything that was once carefree or humdrum? Perhaps he had. I had learned, from Ion Rohrlich among others, that determined jauntiness in certain souls often camouflages misery. This William, Bill or Billy might be one of them.

'I am Dinu Grigorescu. I am Romanian by birth, French by choice, and English by accident.'

I was cheerfully drunk. It was in a mood of drunken cheerfulness that I invited the stranger to come home with me. If this was the act of a madman, then so be it, I reasoned.

I lit the gas fire in my sitting room. It spluttered, as it always did, before it coughed its reluctant way into flame.

'I would advise you to keep your coat on until the room warms up.'

'I'm not cold.'

'You should be. What do I call you?'

'Let's settle for Billy.'

I was Dinu for him – not Dinicu; not Dinuleț.

'May I offer you whisky or red wine?'

'No beer?'

'No beer.'

'I've never had wine.'

'Try some.'

'I want you first. I really and truly want you first.'

What happened next confounds my memory still. We kissed; we embraced; we undressed in a frenzy. I was no longer Dinu Grigorescu, the prince's boy's boy, but someone quite other. I could not recognize myself in the excited flurry. I was flesh and blood and little else.

There had been no time for navigation, I thought as I lay beside him after our passion had abated – no time at all.

'I needed that, Dinu.'

I was tempted to say 'So did I', but couldn't. What had happened was an unexpected gift, a Christmas present of a distinctly unusual kind.

'I should like to stay with you till morning.'

I brought him a glass of claret, which he clearly didn't enjoy drinking. He pulled a disgusted face.

'Give me some water, will you?'

Billy Hawkins, from London's Clapton, was an invader rather than an explorer or navigator. I smiled at the silly conceit that he was an Attila compared with Răzvan's Marco Polo. I was happy enough to be conquered, though it was impossible to imagine Billy as a lasting lover. I didn't want a lasting lover, anyway.

'You are beautiful.' It was Billy speaking.

'Not any more, I fear. I am fifty-six. How old are you?'

'Twenty-seven. I am attracted – deeply attracted, in case you hadn't noticed – to mature men.'

I doubted, I very much doubted, I said, that I was mature. I neglected to add that there were times when I seemed to be perpetually youthful. I was the skinny boy in Paris, in the summer of 1927, with his improbable literary ambitions, whose affections my mother and Răzvan continued to fight over, with no one the winner, in the dreamful darkness of Marylebone.

I made coffee for my unlikely-looking Attila, who had dropped his conqueror's manner in favour of something more feminine, more vulnerable.

'Who is that man in the photograph?'

'He is Răzvan Popescu. He was, and is, my lover. He died before the war.'

'He looks a bit like me.'

'Yes, Billy, he does look a bit like you. And there the resemblance ends.'

'Was he as good as me in bed?'

'You thought you were good in bed, did you?'

'You know I was. You know so. I sent you crazy, crazy, crazy, Dinu.'

'Yes, you did,' I said, honestly.

'So was he as good as Billy Hawkins?'

'He was different. Please don't ask me why. He was different.'

That was all I could say, and that had been more than enough already.

I have not seen Billy Hawkins again. There were times I craved his company – his sexual company, to be correct – and was tempted to phone him, but I desisted. He was an amiable young man, with whom I might have had a liaison, of a kind. It was the caveat 'of a kind' that prevented me opening what was left of my heart to him. He was too young for me, though he insisted that I was just the right age to keep him happy. I sensed, on the morning of December 21, that he had only his body to share with me. He lacked, pleasant as he was, what we Romanians know as *sufletul*: a soul. It was a word you only heard in churches in London, whereas Răzvan and I, at our most contented, used it without embarrassment, often. I feared giving Billy the chance to prove to me that he possessed the depths of sadness and doubt that made the prince's boy so abidingly attractive to me.

I'd poured him a second cup of coffee and watched him eat buttered toast topped with the Dundee marmalade I had first enjoyed with Amalia some thirty years before. It had been one of the many delicacies she had bought on the account my father kept at Dragomir.

'We are breaking the law, Billy. We are criminals. We could be sent to prison,' I said as we kissed goodbye.

'I like living dangerously. It's more fun that way.'

Then I thanked him for the night of bliss we had had together.

'You were pretty good yourself. It takes two to tango.'

I closed the door behind him and returned to the dishevelled bed we had abandoned two hours ago. I lay back and paid homage to Răzvan with my now slightly liver-spotted right hand.

My cousin Eduard, who had introduced me to the art of the free spirit that was Josephine Baker in Paris in 1927, was shot dead by a firing squad in the company of unrepentant Fascists. This I knew from my work as a translator for the World Service. Of my father's fate, of Amalia's, of Elisabeta's, I was still, to my misfortune, completely ignorant. They had been absorbed into a general anonymity, consigned to the nothingness of subjugation. They were as good as ghosts to me now.

They were brought back to life, or something like it, when my secretary announced that Ciprian Văduva wished to speak to me. It was with trepidation that I instructed her to show him into my tiniest of offices at the university. Ciprian? Văduva? I wondered exactly who he was.

'Good afternoon, Professor Grigorescu. I am the son of Elisabeta and George Văduva, the poet you have rescued from oblivion. I am more than happy to meet you at last.'

We shook hands. I invited him to sit down.

'It was not too difficult tracing you. I am pleased to see you alive and well. My mother sends you kisses.'

'How is she?'

'She survives. That is her word, Professor. She has willed herself to survive.'

'Do you still live with her?'

'We are inseparable. She would have me leave home and marry, but I cannot do so, yet.'

I asked him where home was. It had been in Basle, but now it was in Paris, of course, the refuge if not hiding place of despairing Romanians. He was, if anything, a Parisian. He spoke his native language, but had never visited his birthplace.

'My mother wanted me to appreciate my father's poetry. I think it defies translation.'

'I think so, too.'

'My mother has taught me to love and forgive him. It has been a long and difficult lesson.'

I could not imagine the spoiled and skittish Elisabeta as a teacher of almost anything remotely interesting. But then I was picturing her as she was before she met and fell in love with George. I saw them again at the first night of *Tristan und Isolde*, their ears indifferent to the glorious music, their eyes fixed glowingly on each other's comeliness. Perhaps her seriousness, her stoicism, had its inspiration in his cruel way of dying.

'She liked to joke that she was a widow even before she became one. Doamna Văduva – Mrs Widow. Do you remember him, Professor Grigorescu ?'

'I shall remember him better if you call me Dinu.'

'Then I shall definitely call you Dinu, Professor.'

'Your father was a shy and modest man. He was diffident about showing his poems to anyone. Your mother contrived to make him show them to me. I thought then, and I think now, that they are exquisite. He has left enough of them for generations to delight in. Forgive me, Ciprian, for sounding professorial.'

'Do I look like him? Do I resemble him in any way?'

'You want me to say yes, don't you?'

'My mother says I am the image of him.'

He wasn't, as far as I could recall.

'You have his nose and his prominent ears.'

'Thank you.'

It was a Friday afternoon. On Friday evenings I always dined at Chez Victor, at the table set aside for me.

'Could you bear to eat French food? You must have it all the time.'

He replied that he would be honoured to dine with his father's champion. So that's who I was. I knew my place, had known it for decades. I lived in the shadows cast by genius.

The greatest Hamlet of his time was seated in his usual place, dining with the greatest Falstaff. Ion Rohrlich and I had marvelled at their performances, during and after the war. Hamlet gave me his customary nod of recognition as the two of them went off to appear in a play they had both confessed they had trouble understanding.

'You have more news concerning my family, haven't you, Ciprian?'

'Yes, I have.'

'I am waiting to hear it, patiently.'

'Did you know that Amalia is still alive?'

'That is very good news. That is the best news you could have brought me.'

'She is not well, Dinu. She has lapses of memory that sometimes go on for days. It's then that she believes my mother is no one closer to her than a nurse, and screams at her to do her job properly. When she is lucid, she calls her daughter Elisabeta and complains about the nurse who had been caring for her. If you met her, there is a chance that she would not recognize you. She is either garrulous or silent, depending on her mood.'

'I have discovered how my cousin, Eduard Vasiliu, died. Is Cezar Grigorescu alive? I should like to know.'

'I cannot answer your question. I assume he must be dead. He disappeared, Dinu. He simply disappeared.'

'Complicatedly, Ciprian, not simply. Nothing he did was simple.'

'Do you have no affection for him?'

'I wish I had. I sincerely wish I had. I cannot warm to him. It upsets me more than I can say that I see no reason, no earthly reason, to warm to him.'

'You had a tangible, living father to love or hate,' Ciprian remarked after a considered silence.

I could do nothing but agree.

I made two suggestions over the meal that evening, both of which delighted the young engineer. The first was that he might attend, in a silent, anonymous capacity if he wished, a lecture I would give the following Tuesday on the poetry of George Văduva, and the second was that I should take a weekend trip to Paris. I had a present for his mother, whom I longed to see again, and to pay my respects to Amalia, my very-far-from-wicked stepmother, if she was lucid enough to accept them. I did not express my sudden, impulsive longing to tend my lover's grave – to remove the weeds that had sprouted over it, I imagined, and to replace them with fresh flowers.

'Cognac, I think?' I heard myself say, and there was the

solicitous Eduard of 1927 opposite me for a second. 'Would you care for a cognac, Ciprian?'

'Yes, I think I would. My mother forewarned me to expect kindness and courtesy from her stepbrother. Is there such a person as a step-uncle, Dinu?'

'I imagine so. If there is, then you are my step-nephew. They do sound cumbersome, don't they?'

Fifteen students attended my lecture on George Văduva. They were already seated – notebooks open; pens poised – when the poet's modest son sneaked in and placed himself in the back row.

I treated the class to a history lesson first. I spoke of the two years at the close of the 1920s when Romania had an infant king on her shaky throne, due to the fact that his priapic father, the rightful sovereign, had put love or lust before duty. That father, King Carol the Second, had regained the even shakier throne in 1930, and from then on Romania swiftly asserted herself as one of the foremost beasts of a bestial Europe. The unlikeliest men and women became apostles of Nazism: hitherto distinguished philosophers and essayists; novelists and poets; dramatists, actors, painters. Adolf Hitler was their saviour, with Goebbels, Göring, Ribbentrop and Hess their Matthew, Mark, Luke and John. The gospels of venomous hatred were written and read in the land.

But not by George Văduva. He contented himself, in his discontented fashion, with unimportant matters like swallows darkening the sky before the onset of spring or music playing in a distant room or a dead woman commenting sadly, but with traces of bitterness, on her husband's imminent funeral. His poems survive because they were not immediately popular or controversial. They seemed to say absolutely nothing relevant to the major issues of the time. They are neither public nor determinedly private, for their imagery is commonplace – so commonplace, in truth, as to invite rejection and dismissal. The very few critics who bothered to review his poetry were united in their contempt. They made play with his name. 'These are the verses of a melancholic widow' wrote one, who signed himself simply Valentin, while others were even more confidently abusive. 'These poems are a widow's weeds sprouting in a pestilential garden' and 'George Văduva's funeral baked meats leave a sour taste on the Romanian palate.'

Lyricists are said not to be political. Petrarch, Dowland, Keats and Leopardi seem to have nothing more than unhappiness to share with their readers. Yet their sorrows are eternal, reflecting as they do the unspoken sadnesses to which we all are prone. It wasn't Văduva's intention to be subversive, but it is possible to regard him as a dissident. A hand captured in a moment of tenderness has more lasting resonance than has a Nazi salute. When Auden observes that poetry makes nothing happen he is both right and wrong. When a heart is stirred to depths of feeling hitherto unregarded, something is happening. Great poetry has the power to deepen our awareness of the transience of life. It takes an inordinate amount of literary courage to write with delicacy, and that is what Văduva did. He was brave enough to concern himself with fragile things and that, paradoxically, is his strength. He has a secure place among the melancholic immortals.

The inconspicuous Ciprian said nothing during my encomium and the reading of his father's lyrics by two of my brightest students that followed. He neither smiled nor wept. He did not introduce himself, as others might have done, as the offspring of a genius.

'I should like to drink a whole pint of strong English beer,' he said to me when the celebration was over.

I accompanied Ciprian on his brief tour of the sights of London. He had seen the Tower and the Houses of Parliament on newsreels and picture postcards, and neither seemed to impress him. It was in the City itself that he became animated. He was bewitched by the churches designed by Wren and Hawksmoor, as Răzvan would have been had he lived to be at my side in my half-life. Ciprian shared his grandmother's scorn for religion, but that distaste of piety evaporated in the face of pure architectural symmetry in Wren and contained disorder in the work of Hawksmoor. An engineer, he reminded me, is an aesthete, too.

Elisabeta had never remarried. She was content to remain Mme Veuve, she joked. What with Ciprian and Amalia to raise and care for, she had had no room or time for another husband. She had counted her blessings, such as they were.

'I have brought you a present.'

'What is it, Dinu? A box of chocolates? Is it a bottle of perfume or cologne?'

'Nothing so mundane.'

'You are being mischievous.'

She was right. I *was* being mischievous. I was about to give her the pearl necklace Prince Radziwill had bestowed upon the golden beauty who was the young Albert Le Cuziat. I'd had no cause or reason to wear it in the thirty years it had been in my bemused possession – no sensible cause or reason at all. I handed it to her in the paper, faded now, in which Albert had wrapped it for me.

'Please accept this, dear Elisabeta, and please wear it.'

She unwrapped the necklace and stared at it, aghast.

'It is very beautiful, Dinu. These are genuine pearls. This isn't costume jewellery. Where did you buy it?'

Her question inspired me to tell the biggest lie I had ever told.

'It was given to me by my mother.' I was shocked by what I had said, but continued without shame. 'On her deathbed.'

'Was it a gift from Cezar Grigorescu? If it was, I do not think I wish to have it.'

Oh, the necessary, fiendish nature of deception. 'Her parents gave it to her on her wedding day.'

'Then I shall accept it happily, my dear sweet stepbrother. Put it round my neck.'

I did so, and felt neither dear nor sweet. I had defamed Elena's spirit by pretending that this token of a rich man's lust for a pretty footman had once belonged to her. It had been a fixture in Albert's Vatican Library, that room for reflection on all matters carnal and snobbish. If those pearls had had ears, they would have hopped and skipped at the sounds coming from the cubicles. On Wednesday afternoons, when Safarov had reduced the wealthy industrialist to a contentedly blood-stained wreck, they would have become balletic. This vision of improbably lively, dancing pearls was with me as I adorned my stepsister with the surprising present Albert had elected to give me – a present in no way comparable to that of Honoré or Răzvan, which I had received from him, at the cost of a hundred francs, to my lasting gratitude on that woozy afternoon in May 1927.

'Come and see Amalia. She has days when she knows who I am and days when she doesn't. She may not recognize you, Dinu. Sometimes she mistakes Ciprian for a tradesman or a delivery boy. Her body is resilient but her mind is unstable.'

She was sitting in an armchair by her bed wearing a dress that Leon Becker, who had been slaughtered in an abattoir in 1941, made for her from a design by Coco Chanel. It hung loosely on her, where once her generous frame had filled it. She was emaciated now but strangely lovely to my eyes, in that simple outfit she had worn on the hateful evening when Eduard and my treacherous father had railed against the perniciousness of the Jewish race.

'Do you know who I am, Amalia?'

'Should I know who you are?'

'I am your stepson Dinu. I am not as pretty as I was when you dressed me in velvet.'

'Were you a pretty boy then?'

'You said I was. You told me often enough I was.'

'Are you the one I dressed in velvet?'

'Yes, I am. Yes, I was.'

'Why did I do that?'

'You know the reason, not me.'

'Do I?'

I took her hand and pressed it. I kissed it, in the Romanian fashion.

'I married your father for his money. Why else would I have married him?'

She sounded sepulchral. She sounded as if she were stating the truth from inside a tomb.

'He must have charmed you,' I said, in my father's defence. 'He must have had some appeal for you.'

'I needed a roof over my head. I needed a home for my daughter, and he needed a mascot.'

'I have seen Rudolf Peterson, Amalia. He has been resident in London for a long time.'

'Who?'

'Rudolf Peterson, the great Romanian tenor. I see him at concert halls with a young man who people say is his nephew.'

'Rudi?'

'He looks very fragile.'

I remembered a conversation I'd had with the still alluring Amalia in September 1935, on the eve of my return to Paris.

'Have you read yesterday's *Figaro*?'

'Not yet, Dinu. Is there something in it that will interest me?'

'Yes, there is.'

It interested her as much as it stimulated me. In the interview with a music critic, the 'shining star of operetta', as he was labelled, to his considerable distaste, asserted that he would not be singing in Romania, Austria and Germany. There was a foul stench emanating from certain parts of Europe and he had no desire to inhale it. The critic had interrupted with the reminder that he, M. Peterson, was not Jewish, which crass observation had inspired the singer to laughter, and when he had done laughing to say: 'I am not a Jew, but the circumstance of my birth does not prevent me being concerned and compassionate. "Some of my best friends are Jewish" is a cliché that has particular resonance for me. The air in London, despite the November fog and the poverty and a few fools in black shirts, is more congenial to my sensitive nostrils.'

'There speaks the man who has broken a dozen hearts, including mine,' Amalia had commented.

It was ironical, was it not, that Elisabeta should be in love with a man named Văduva, the Romanian word for 'widow'? Her own romance with Rudi or Rudolf – he was Rudi in the bedroom and Rudolf on the stage – had happened when he was appearing as Danilo in *The Merry Widow*.

'My poor daughter has not been the merriest of widows. M. Văduva saw to that,' she said, again sepulchrally.

'Be quiet, Mamă. Talk to Dinu about other things.'

I knew from what Ciprian had told me in London that Amalia, Elisabeta and the little Văduva had lived in Basle throughout the war. When money became scarce, Elisabeta had given piano lessons to the children of the rich. Of Cezar's whereabouts they had known nothing and knew nothing still.

'Do you want to make your peace with him?' Amalia asked, staring at me.

I hesitated.

'Yes, I do, if only for my mother's sake. My mother would rest contented if I made peace with him.'

Her eyes lost their dullness. They glittered as she said: 'Are you telling me your sainted mother isn't happy among her angels and cherubs? She ought to be. She damned well ought to be. She was spared years of his meanness and cynicism. She made the great escape from him. I wish I had. I live in fear that he will find me. Elena is beyond his reach, because if he is dead he is sure to be in hell.'

'Stop it, Mamă. You are upsetting Dinu.'

'No, no,' I protested. 'I sympathize with what your mother says.'

'How is the prince's boy? Is he being kind to you?'

'He died, Mamă.'

'Did he? How thoughtless of him. So Dinu is a widow as well?'

'I am, Amalia. I have been widowed, in a manner of speaking, for thirty years.'

'You looked so ravishing in velvet, my love. I was tempted to eat you up. Come and live with us. We could be such a happy family – you, me, Elisabeta and Ciprian.'

'I should like that,' I said. I was speaking the truth. I should have liked to live with them, impossible though the prospect was.

'It will not be for a long time, Dinu. I am dying, my sweet.'

'You are not dying,' said Ciprian. Those were the only words he spoke.

I knew, beyond all doubt, that she would outlive me. I had weeks to live. In her eyes, my paleness was that of the Dinu she had cosseted and cooed over in another time, in another country. She was not to know that it was now the pallor of impending death.

I might have said as much to her, but nodded and smiled instead. I was Elena's son, and could not be honest with her. I elected to stay silent.

I kissed her cheeks and hands. I said *au revoir*. I had work to do in London. I hoped to see her later in the year, I heard myself lying.

We have words at our command but it is often wise not to voice them. Silence was my parting gift to Amalia, my second mother, my witty sharer of precious secrets.

I entered the churchyard, anemones in hand, to search for Răzvan's grave. I anticipated that it would be difficult to find after thirty years. Many others had been buried here since that bleak afternoon in March 1937. Perhaps the gravestone had gone, or perhaps it was blackened beyond recognition, his name and dates of birth and death obliterated or covered up with rampantly growing ivy. I expected weeds and that curious damp decay one senses and smells in neglected cemeteries. The weeds and ivy were there in abundance, but nowhere near Răzvan's resting place. The white marble I had chosen was as white as I remembered it. Someone had washed, or even polished it regularly. And someone had planted a fern behind it. And someone had left fresh tulips in an elegant blue vase on the well-trimmed grass that was his plot. Someone had been attentive to him for all the time since his death, it seemed. I became no one as I stared at a display of loving neatness and order that bewildered and hurt me.

I had been jealous of the prince and Răzvan's clients in 1927, when I was nineteen and overflowing with unconsidered love. I was jealous again now, insanely so, of a someone I had neither the will nor the energy to track down. Who was he? He had not been in the hospital during Răzvan's final illness, for mine was a constant vigil. Who was he? Who in hell was he?

I had not eaten for hours, but there was bile inside me and out it came. I besmirched his grave with a hideous, blood-flecked yellowness that was, in those few anguished moments, all that was left in me of love. My lungs ached and my legs were signalling that they were on the verge of collapsing beneath me.

I made sure there was nobody else in the graveyard before I surrendered myself to the long-abandoned luxury of weeping.

*

'I warned you,' she chided me in Marylebone. 'You will die without his love.'

I invited Răzvănel to disagree with her, but he said nothing.

It distressed me to think they had stopped arguing. I had found their bickering oddly comforting. I had been consoled by their possessiveness on those nights in wartime London when the blackout had made the darkness darker. Seventeen years of death divided them, and I had lived in all that time with their concern for me.

'Did you hear what I said to you?'

'I did, Mamă.'

'If you confess your sins, *mon petit*, I will speak to you as I spoke to you when you were my beautiful, God-fearing son.'

'Will you?'

'You have my promise, Dinicu.'

She had taken her name for me back from Răzvan. I wanted it to be his only.

'I am sick of being called beautiful,' I declared, not just to Elena, not just to Răzvan, not just to Albert Le Cuziat, and not just to Amalia and Elisabeta. I begged the whole wide world to rescue me from its curse.

The whole wide world, unsurprisingly, did not respond to my request.

'Are you a virgin, Jean-Pierre?'

I said nothing, as before.

'That means yes.'

'Yes.'

'There is no someone, Dinu. There never was, and never will be, a someone. How could you doubt me? You should be ashamed for being so jealous.'

'I am, Răzvănel, I am.'

'The monster is leading you astray again, you fool,' shrieked my mother.

'He wants to be led astray. It was his one great wish. I gratified that wish.'

'You fiend.'

'You saint.'

They were back in their loving business, I realized soon after waking. I could die now in some contentment, before hostilities were ended and a truce was called.

I am sitting on Mme Proust's chaise longue as I wait to learn from Albert Le Cuziat if the man I know cannot be called Honoré will be free to explore Jean-Pierre again. It is a sunlit day in Paris, much like the day it is in London forty years later. I am both here and there. I am the man who gave himself to the prince's boy and the nervous youth who will hear in an hour's time that Răzvan has fallen in love with Dinu. Perhaps it is the shot of pain-killing morphine that allows my past and my present to intermingle so happily.

Răzvan wanted to write a memoir with the title The Prince's Boy, telling the story of the rich man who cared for him like the most beneficent of fathers for a few enchanted, surprising years. Here is The Prince's Boy once more, written by one who met his lifetime's lover in unromantic surroundings – not by a tennis court or at a party but in a cubicle in a brothel near rue l'Arcade.

I am bequeathing this collection of memories and reflections to Ciprian Văduva, another fatherless son. I hope he will be enlightened by what he reads.

Acknowledgements

I WISH TO express my abiding gratitude to the doctors and nurses in the Cardiac Unit at Hammersmith Hospital, London, and to thank the Committee of the Royal Literary Fund for their continuing support. Dr Kamal Winayak and his four assistants – Pauline, Irene, Sue and Irma – at the Ashchurch Medical Centre offered support of a different, but necessary, kind. Michael Fishwick, Deborah Rogers, Anna Simpson, Mohsen Shah and the irrepressible Bill Payne have been especially helpful. My thanks to the heroic Bill Pashley, that model of fortitude, and to the considerate Raúl Sánchez Pérez. I offer my respects to the brave, good-humoured Romanians I have been fortunate to know – the wonderful Antoaneta Ralian, still translating in her ninth decade, is their representative here. I could not have written this book without the encouragement of Jeremy Trevathan, the best of best friends.